She separated herself from the others and met him halfway.

"I wasn't expecting the special agent I requested to be you," Madison spoke in clear shock.

Garrett grinned awkwardly. "Surprise." He thought about giving her a quick hug, if only for old times' sake. Being able to make body contact wouldn't be bad either. But he sensed it would be an inappropriate gesture at this time.

A hand rested on a hip of her slender frame as she questioned, "So, how long have you been back in this region?"

Was there any right way to answer her? "Not long. I was planning to call you."

"Right." Her curly lashes fluttered cynically. "Anyway, this isn't about us," she stressed, for which he concurred. "Someone I know has been murdered and we need to work together to solve the crime."

To H. Loraine, the love of my life and best friend, whose support has been unwavering through the many wonderful years together. To my dear mother, Marjah Aljean, who gave me the tools to pursue my passions in life, including writing fiction for publication; and for my loving sister, Jacquelyn, who helped me become the person I am today, along the way. To the loyal fans of my romance, mystery, suspense and thriller fiction published over the years. Lastly, a nod goes out to my wonderful editors, Allison Lyons and Denise Zaza, for the great opportunity to lend my literary voice and creative spirit to the successful Intrigue line.

MURDER IN THE BLUE RIDGE MOUNTAINS

———

R. Barri Flowers

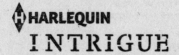

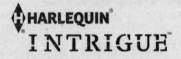

ISBN-13: 978-1-335-59149-4

Murder in the Blue Ridge Mountains

Recycling programs
for this product may
not exist in your area.

For questions and comments about the quality of this book,
please contact us at CustomerService@Harlequin.com.

Harlequin Enterprises ULC
22 Adelaide St. West, 41st Floor
Toronto, Ontario M5H 4E3, Canada
www.Harlequin.com

Printed in U.S.A.

R. Barri Flowers is an award-winning author of crime, thriller, mystery and romance fiction featuring three-dimensional protagonists, riveting plots, unexpected twists and turns, and heart-pounding climaxes. With an expertise in true crime, serial killers and characterizing dangerous offenders, he is perfectly suited for the Harlequin Intrigue line. Chemistry and conflict between the hero and heroine, attention to detail and incorporating the very latest advances in criminal investigations are the cornerstones of his romantic suspense fiction. Discover more on popular social networks and Wikipedia.

Books by R. Barri Flowers

Harlequin Intrigue

The Lynleys of Law Enforcement

Special Agent Witness
Christmas Lights Killer
Murder in the Blue Ridge Mountains

Hawaii CI

The Big Island Killer
Captured on Kauai
Honolulu Cold Homicide
Danger on Maui

Chasing the Violet Killer

Visit the Author Profile page at Harlequin.com.

CAST OF CHARACTERS

Madison Lynley—A law enforcement ranger who goes after a serial killer on the Blue Ridge Parkway, while having to work with a former boyfriend assigned to the case. Can they put aside their differences to solve crime and rediscover each other?

Garrett Sneed—A national park service special agent who finds the death of young women eerily similar to his mother's murder in the Blue Ridge Mountains thirty years ago. Could there be a connection? And, with the help of the woman he mistakenly walked away from, can the Cherokee investigator uncover it?

Nicole Wallenberg—A park ranger involved in the investigation and trying to avoid becoming a victim.

Ward Wilcox—A park maintenance ranger who seems to be caught in the middle of the case. Does he have something to hide?

Ray Pottenger—A deputy sheriff assisting in the serial killer investigation and equally determined to solve it.

Blue Ridge Parkway Killer—The unsub is stabbing women on the Parkway to death and has set his sights on a certain pretty law enforcement ranger... Can he be stopped?

Prologue

Jessica Sneed was a proud member of the Eastern Band of Cherokee Indians, a tribe based in North Carolina. But she was even prouder of being the mother to a rambunctious little dark-haired boy named Garrett. Being a single parent at age twenty-five was anything but easy. Had it been up to her, she would be happily wed with a strong marriage foundation and Garrett would have both parents to dote on him. That wasn't the case, though, as his father, Andrew Crowe, wasn't much interested in being a husband. Much less a dad. Besieged with alcohol-related issues and a self-centered attitude, he'd left the state two years ago, abandoning her, forcing Jessica to go it alone in taking care of her then three-year-old son. Well, maybe not entirely alone, as her parents, Trevor and Dinah Sneed, did their best to help out whenever they could.

Shamelessly, Jessica took full advantage of the precious little time she had to herself, such as this sunny afternoon when she got to hike in the Blue Ridge Mountains. She loved being in touch with na-

ture and giving back to the land her forefathers had
once roamed freely, through retracing their footsteps
in paying her respects. She made sure that Garrett,
whom she'd given her family surname, was aware
of his rich heritage as well. They spent some time
in the mountains and forest together when he wasn't
in school.

But today, it's just me, Jessica told herself as she ran
a hand down the length of her waist-long black hair,
worn in a bouffant ponytail. She was wearing tennis
shoes along with a T-shirt and cuffed denim shorts on
the warm August day as she trekked across the hiking trail on the Blue Ridge Parkway, the hundreds-
of-miles-long scenic roadway that meandered through
the mountains. She stopped for a moment to enjoy some
shade beneath the Raven Rocks Overlook and took a
bottle of water from her backpack.

After opening it, Jessica drank half the bottle and
returned it to the backpack. She was about to get on
her way when she heard a sound. She wondered if it
might be coming from wildlife, such as a chipmunk
or red squirrel. She had even noticed wild turkey and
white-tailed deer roaming around. Humans had to
adapt more than the other way around. Some did.
Others chose not to.

She heard another noise coming from the woods,
this one heavier. Suddenly feeling concerned that it
could mean danger, Jessica headed back in the direction from which she'd come.

But the sounds grew louder, echoing all around
her, and seemed to be getting closer and closer. Was

it a wild animal that had targeted her? Perhaps rabid and ravenous? Should she make a run for it? Or stay still and pray that the threat would leave her alone? As she grappled with these thoughts, Jessica dared to glance over her shoulder at the potential menace. It was not an animal predator. But a human one. It was a man. He was dark haired, with ominous even-darker eyes and a scowl on his face. In one large hand was a long-bladed knife.

Her heart racing like crazy, Jessica turned away from him to run but pivoted so quickly that she lost her balance and the backpack slipped from her shoulders. She fell flat onto the dirt pathway, hitting her head hard against it. Seeing stars, she tried to clear her brain and, at the same time, get up. Before she could, she felt the knife plunge deep into her back. The pain was excruciating. But it got much worse as he stabbed her again and again, till the pain seemed to leave her body, along with the will to live. What hurt even more was not getting to say goodbye to her son. She silently asked Garrett for forgiveness in not being around for him before complete darkness and a strange peace hit Jessica all at once.

HE TOOK A moment to study the lifeless body on the ground before him. Killing her had been even more gratifying than he had imagined in his wildest dreams. He recalled his mother once telling him as a child that he was messed up in the head. The memory made him want to laugh. Yes, she'd been right. He had to agree that he wasn't all there where it concerned being

good and bad, much more preferring the latter over
the former. His sorry excuse of a mother had found
out firsthand that getting on his bad side came with
dire consequences. Too bad for her that he'd put her
out of her misery and made sure no one ever caught
on that he'd been responsible for her untimely death.

His eyes gazed upon the corpse again. How lucky
for him that she'd happened upon his sight at just the
right place and time when the desire to kill had struck
his fancy. It had been almost too perfect. A pretty
lamb had come to him for her slaughter. He wondered
what had been going through her head as she'd lain
dying, a knife wedged deep inside her back. Maybe it
had only been his imagination, but there had almost
seemed to be a ray of light in her big brown eyes before they'd shut for good, as though she'd been seeing something or someone out of his reach.

He grabbed the knife with his gloved hand and
flung it into the flowering shrubs. There were plenty
more where that had come from. And he intended
to make good use of them. Too bad for the next one
to feel the sting of his sharp blade. But that wasn't
his concern. A man had to do what a man had to do.
And nothing and no one would stop him.

He grinned crookedly and walked away from the
dead woman, soon disappearing into the woods,
where he would slip back into his normal life. Before the time came for a repeat performance.

Chapter One

Thirty years later, Law Enforcement Ranger Madison Lynley drove her Chevrolet Tahoe Special Service Vehicle along the Blue Ridge Parkway in the Pisgah Ranger District of Pisgah National Forest, where she was stationed in North Carolina. It was a gorgeous span of nearly five hundred miles of scenery that ran through the Blue Ridge Mountains.

She had been employed as a law enforcement ranger with the National Park Service for the past eight years, or since she'd been twenty-seven, after completing four months of basic training. Along with receiving her bachelor's degree in natural resource ecology and management and a master's degree in environmental science from Oklahoma State University. In the process, she had chosen to go in a different direction than her brothers, Scott and Russell, who were both FBI special agents, as well as their adopted younger sister, Annette, who was a sheriff's department detective. All of them had followed in the footsteps of their parents, Taylor and Caroline Lynley, with long careers in law enforcement. Their father had been a chief of police with the Oklahoma City Police Department, while her mother had once been an Oklahoma County District Court criminal judge.

The fact that both were now deceased pained Madison, as they'd been the rocks of the family, leaving it to their children to carry on without them. All seemed more than committed to doing just that, remaining fairly close, in spite of each going their separate ways in adulthood as they navigated their lives, careers and other interests.

In full uniform on a slender five-eight frame, Madison continued to drive. She admired the forest—rich in chestnut oak, birch and buckeye trees—on this late summer day. As one of only a relatively small number of rangers patrolling the more than eighty thousand acres of land along the parkway, she never tired of this, loving the freedom and appreciation of nature and wildlife the job provided. Beyond patrolling the park in her vehicle, she had also ridden on bicycles, snowmobiles, ATVs, boats and even horses in the course of the job. She had participated in search-and-rescue missions, dealt with car accidents, wildfires and dangerous or wounded animals, you name it.

Then there was the criminal activity, such as illicit drug use, drug dealing and occasional crimes of violence that forced Madison into the law enforcement part of being a ranger. She was equipped with a Sig Sauer P320 semiautomatic pistol in her duty holster, should she need it when having to deal with hostile and dangerous park visitors.

Thank goodness I've never had to shoot anyone

yet, she thought, while knowing there was always a first time for everything.

Madison's mind turned to her love life. Or lack thereof. She was now thirty-five years old, nearly thirty-six, and still very much single. She couldn't even remember the last time she had gone out on a real date. Actually, she could. It was two years ago when she'd been dating Garrett Sneed, a handsome Cherokee special agent with the National Park Service Investigative Services Branch. For a few months there, they'd been hot and heavy and had appeared headed for bigger and better things. And then, just like that, it had been over, as though it had never begun.

She couldn't really put a finger on why they'd broken up. Only that neither had seemed ready to make a real commitment to each other and the opportunity to fix things that had gone unsaid or undone had slipped through the cracks. Before she could even think about trying to get back together, Garrett had gotten a transfer to another region, as though he couldn't leave soon enough. They'd lost touch from that point on, leaving Madison to wonder about what might have been if they had tried harder.

When she got a call over the radio, Madison snapped out of the reverie and responded. It was her boss, Tom Hutchison.

"Hey," he spoke in a tense voice, "we just got a report of a dead woman discovered by a hiker along the Blue Ridge Parkway."

"Hmm…not a great way to start the day," Madison muttered, never wanting to hear that a life had been lost, whatever the circumstances. "Are we talking about an accident, suicide, animal attack or...?"

"Could be any of the above." Hutchison was vague. "Check it out and make your own assessment. We'll go from there."

"I'm on my way," she said tersely, after being given the location.

As was the case any time she had to deal with a death, all types of things went through Madison's head. Who was the victim, and why had the person been at the park? Was this something that could have been prevented, such as the taking of one's own life? Or was it the result of actions beyond the control of the deceased, such as an encounter with a black bear? Or a human predator.

Bad news no matter what, Madison told herself frankly. She would soon get some clarity, as she parked her car and was met by an anxious-looking African American woman in her fifties, with curly black crochet braids and hiking attire.

"I'm Ranger Lynley," Madison said. "And you are?"

"Loretta Redmond."

"You found a body?"

"Yeah. While I was hiking, though I nearly missed seeing her where the body was located. I could tell she was dead." Loretta took a deep breath and shook her head in dismay. "I still can't believe it."

Madison understood, as seeing a corpse outside of a funeral setting was something that was hard to forget for most people. "Can you take me to her?"

She followed Loretta through a wooded area and

down a steep embankment, asking, "Did you see anyone else coming or going?"

"No one," Loretta replied without hesitation.

"Okay." Madison was thoughtful as they reached a spot off a trail that was overgrown, where there lay the body of a tall and slim female. She was lying flat on her stomach, wearing a purple-colored sports bra, printed blue running shorts, and white tennis shoes. Blood spilled onto the dirt from several gashes in her back, neck and elsewhere that Madison speculated had come from a long knife. She glanced at the thirtysomething victim's short red hair in a pixie cut with tapering sideburns.

Only then did a sense of familiarity hit Madison like a hard smack in the face. Upon closer inspection of the person's discolored round face that was turned awkwardly to one side, her lids shut, Madison realized with shock that she was looking at her friend and neighbor Olivia Forlani, a brown-eyed attorney from the nearby town of Kiki's Ridge. Both loved to jog and just yesterday had met up on Madison's day off for a run on the popular trail at Pisgah National Forest.

As though sensing her troubled expression, Loretta said, "You look like you've seen a ghost."

Madison swallowed thickly in turning away from Olivia's body. "Worse than that," she remarked, maudlin. "There's nothing supernatural about what's happened here. It's very real. Someone killed her."

Which left Madison wondering who would have done such a horrible thing to her friend. It would be left largely up to the NPS Investigative Services Branch to figure that out. She would need to phone this in and have them get a criminal investigator out there right away, while wondering who would do the honors with Garrett now working on the other side of the country.

All things considered, she believed that was probably for the best as neither of them needed distractions, and her friend's death as a near certain victim of homicide would be the top priority of the ISB agent sent.

"A WOMAN HAS reportedly been stabbed to death on the Blue Ridge Parkway," Carly Tafoya, the recently appointed director of the South Atlantic-Gulf Region of the National Park Service Investigative Services Branch, said glumly.

ISB Special Agent Garrett Sneed cocked a thick brow as the shocking news registered while they stood in his midsize, sparsely furnished office in Region 2, in Atlanta, Georgia, where he was stationed. His sable eyes gazed at the petite green-eyed director who was ten years older than his age of thirty-six but looked younger. She had short brunette hair in an A-line cut and wore a brown pantsuit with black pumps.

"That's terrible," he uttered candidly.

"Tell me about it." She rolled her eyes. "This isn't the way we want to greet visitors to the park. Not by a long shot."

Garrett couldn't have agreed more, as he towered over her at six feet, two and a half inches on a muscular frame. "Who called it in?" he wondered, knowing this was ranger territory.

"Law Enforcement Ranger Madison Lynley," the director replied.

Garrett reacted to this revelation, though having guessed that his ex-girlfriend would be at the center of the investigation, whether he wanted it or not, with the strained history between them. Some things in life simply couldn't be helped.

"Ranger Lynley," he said equably. "We worked together when I was with the region previously."

"Makes sense." Carly nodded. "Apparently a hiker spotted the victim and reported it."

Garrett pinched his nose. "What about the perpetrator?"

"Still on the loose, unfortunately." She frowned. "I'm assigning you this case, Sneed," she told him without preface. "Should be right up your alley. Especially after you recently cracked the Melissa Lafferty case."

He thought briefly about the missing person investigation at the Grand Canyon National Park in northern Arizona. Turned out that the missing twenty-two-year-old Lafferty had been abducted by an ex-boyfriend who'd held her prisoner for weeks in a room at his Phoenix house before she'd been rescued and the kidnapper arrested and charged with multiple offenses. Garrett was happy that though Melissa Lafferty had been put through the ringer, she'd survived, knowing that wasn't always the end result, with the current Blue Ridge Parkway case a sad but true example.

He winced while running a hand through his hair. Eyeing the director squarely, Garrett said painfully, "My mother was murdered in the Blue Ridge Mountains while hiking."

"What? That's awful. I'm sorry to hear that." Carly wrinkled her nose, thoughtful for a beat. "If this hits too close to home, Garrett, I can assign the case to another special agent."

"I've got this," he told her flatly. "It happened a long time ago." Moreover, Garrett knew that with fewer than forty ISB special agents in the entire country under the authority of the NPS, none had the luxury of picking and choosing assignments based on their history or personal circumstances. It was no different with him, even if he had more than one reason for not being enthusiastic to return to North Carolina. "I can be there in three hours," he told her, taking into account normal traffic and speed limits along the way.

"Good." Carly gave him a soft smile. "The sooner you can wrap this up, the sooner we can ease the legitimate concerns of park-goers."

"I agree." In Garrett's mind, it also meant the sooner he could get out of North Carolina and the bad memories he'd left behind, which did not include his prior involvement with Madison. It was perhaps the one bright spot, even if things had ended between them prematurely. At least it seemed that way to him, looking back.

Garrett drove his department-issued silver Chevrolet Tahoe Special Service Vehicle back to his two-bedroom, nicely furnished, nearly a-century-old condominium on Peachtree Street in downtown Atlanta. There, he packed a bag, placed his loaded Glock 23 40 S&W caliber semiautomatic pistol in a shoulder holster, and was out the door.

Soon, he was on I-85 North en route to the Blue Ridge Parkway. Garrett pursed his lips as he thought about the stabbing death of his mother, Jessica Sneed, who'd been part of the Eastern Band of Cherokee Indians, a federally recognized sovereign nation in Western North Carolina. He'd been just five years old at the time, when someone had taken her life that hot summer day thirty years ago. The case had never been solved, and Garrett was forced to live with that haunting reality, blaming himself for not accompanying his mother that day to protect her from a killer. Of course, he'd been too young to have been able to do much to thwart the brutal attack, but he only wished the opportunity had been there to try his hardest to make a difference. After her death, he had been taken in by his maternal grandparents, Trevor and Dinah Sneed, who lived in the Qualla Boundary, land owned by the EBCI and kept in trust by the US government.

When he'd reached adulthood, Garrett had left the Qualla, still stung by the memory of his mother's death. Having never known his father, it had been Garrett's grandparents who'd taught him how to be a proud Cherokee and to fend for himself. He'd attended North Carolina Central University, where he'd gotten his bachelor's degree in criminal justice, before becoming a park ranger and working his way to being an NPS ISB special agent.

Garrett's musings turned to Madison Lynley, an attractive ranger he had fallen hard for. He was pretty sure she'd been equally into him, the few short months they'd been an item. But somehow, the timing had seemed off and they'd broken up. Though it had been mutual and he believed they'd parted on good terms, if that were possible, rather than put pressure on either of them while working in the same space, he'd put in for a transfer to the National Park Service Investigative Services Branch Southwest Region and had been assigned to the Grand Canyon National Park field office. But three months ago, Garrett had been reassigned again to the South Atlantic-Gulf Region, opting to stay in Atlanta and not make things uncomfortable for Madison.

Now he wondered if that had been a mistake. Two years had gone by since he'd last seen her. No texts, emails, phone calls or video chats. Nothing. Had she truly forgotten everything that had existed between them? What about keeping in touch as they had pledged to do? Was he any less guilty of breaking that promise than she was? For his part, if honest about it, Garrett knew that not a day had passed when he hadn't thought about Madison on some level, wondering how she was getting on and if she had moved on with someone else. He had not. Some relationships were hard to substitute, even if they'd failed to progress into something truly meaningful and lasting.

When he arrived at the Blue Ridge Parkway a few hours later, Garrett was admittedly as nervous about seeing Madison again as he was determined to solve the homicide on the parkway. *I'll just have to suck it up and treat this like any other investigation*, he told himself, getting out of the vehicle and approaching a group of law enforcement and personnel from the medical examiner's office. But from the moment he laid eyes on Madison, looking as gorgeous as ever, even in her law enforcement ranger uniform that hid that hot body and with her long and luscious blond hair tucked away in a bun, Garrett knew he had to throw that game plan right out the proverbial window. This would definitely be anything but "any other investigation" as long as she was part of it.

She separated herself from the others and met him halfway, those big pretty blue-green eyes widening quizzically beneath choppy bangs and above a petite nose and full lips on a heart-shaped face.

"I wasn't expecting the ISB special agent I requested to be you," Madison spoke in clear shock. He hadn't decided if it was a good or bad shock on her part.

Garrett grinned awkwardly. "Surprise." He thought about giving her a quick hug, if only for old times' sake. Being able to make body contact wouldn't be bad either. But he sensed it would be an inappropriate gesture at this time.

A hand rested on a hip of her slender frame as she

questioned, "So, how long have you been back in this region?"

Uh-oh, he told himself. Was there any right way to answer her?

"Not long." Garrett took a middle of the road approach. "I was planning to call you," he lied. Though perhaps he would have gotten around to it sooner or later. Or was that just a convenient rationalization for not knowing whether or not it was smart to go there?

"Right." Her curly lashes fluttered cynically. "Anyway, this isn't about us," she stressed, with which he concurred. "Someone I know has been murdered, and we need to work together to solve the crime."

Garrett was caught off guard on the notion that she'd been acquainted with the dead woman, giving him even more incentive to complete the investigation as soon as possible—hopefully leading to an arrest or otherwise preventing the unsub from harming anyone else.

"Sorry to hear that you were connected to the victim, Madison," he voiced sincerely. "Why don't you take me to the body and fill me in on any details you have thus far, and we'll proceed from there."

"Fine," she told him tersely. "Olivia deserves no less than to have whoever did this to her off the streets and behind bars."

Garrett thought back to his mother and her untimely demise. He only wished she had gotten the justice she'd deserved. Maybe this time around it would be a different outcome. "We're in total agreement."

Chapter Two

I almost wish he wasn't still so handsome, Madison thought as she assessed Garrett Sneed, her ex-boyfriend. Had that been the case, it might not be as bad to see him walk back into her life after two years apart. But as it was, if anything, the ISB special agent was actually even more striking than she'd remembered. He had dark eyes, a Nubian nose, prominent cheekbones reflecting his Cherokee heritage and a square jawline on an oval face, with a light stubble beard. The thick dark hair, she realized, was different. Instead of the hipster style he'd worn before, it was now in a mid-fade haircut that suited him. Tall and well-built, he was wearing a short-sleeved green shirt, tan slacks, and a vest that had Police Federal Agent on the back, along with comfortable plain toe Oxfords.

Madison blushed when he caught her studying him, though she had noticed him doing the same in seeing how she'd been holding up since the last time they'd met. Knowing her food-and-exercise regimen, she was confident that she'd passed the test just fine. Assuming he was grading her.

"Follow me," she told him, trying to keep this professional.

"Lead the way," he said evenly.

She introduced him to sheriff's deputies from Transylvania, Buncombe and Watauga Counties and staff from the medical examiner's office before they headed down a well-worn path toward the crime scene.

"This is really hard," Madison commented. "Not exactly the way I expected to meet again."

"I know." Garrett followed close behind her through the grove of trees. "Losing anyone you're connected to is a hard pill to swallow. Not what I was expecting, either, in seeing you again, but duty called for it."

Along with the fact that you just happened to have returned to this region, which made such an unlikely reunion even possible, she thought, feeling his breath as it fell on her skin. She wondered just how long he had been in her neck of the woods and never bothered to get in touch, if only for old times' sake. Or was that really necessary, considering that things had ended for them and there was no going back?

She came upon the area that had been cordoned off with yellow tape and had crime scene investigators searching for and collecting evidence. Weaving her way through with Garrett, who flashed his identification as the lead investigator but unfamiliar to some at work, they headed down the steep embankment to where the decedent was located beneath dense brush.

Madison gulped. "There she is." It pained her to see what was once a living, breathing, healthy human being now a murder victim. On hand was Deputy Chief Medical Examiner Dawn Dominguez. The fortysomething doctor was small boned and had brunette hair in a stacked pixie.

"Long time no see, Special Agent Sneed," Dawn remarked as she planted brown eyes upon Garrett.

"It's been a minute, Doc," he allowed.

"Sorry you had to be brought back in under these circumstances."

"So am I. But it comes with the territory." Garrett favored Madison with an even look and returned to eyeing the victim. "What can you tell us?"

Dawn, who was wearing nitrile gloves while conducting a preliminary examination of the body, responded, "Well, my initial read is that the decedent was the victim of a multiple-stabbing attack, resulting in her death."

His brow furrowed. "Any defensive wounds?"

"None that I can see thus far. It appears as though the assailant caught her by surprise and from behind before going on the attack."

Madison anguished over the thought of her friend's painful victimization and agonizing end to her life. "What was the estimated time of death?"

Dawn took a moment or two to contemplate and answered, "I have to say she's probably been dead for anywhere from four to six hours. I'll know more when the autopsy is completed."

"Any indication of a sexual assault?" she had to ask, even if Olivia was fully clothed.

"Doesn't appear to be the case. Again, I can be more definitive after the autopsy."

"The sooner I can get that report, the better," Garrett stressed.

"Understood," the medical examiner said. "We all want to get to the bottom of this."

Madison nodded in concurrence, while hopeful that Olivia hadn't suffered the further indignity of a sexual victimization in the course of losing her life.

After the decedent was put in a body bag, placed onto a gurney and wheeled to the medical examiner's van, Garrett asked Madison, "Any sign of the murder weapon?"

"Our initial search has turned up nothing," she told him, wishing that weren't the case. "Hopefully, the CSIs will find the knife used in the attack." But truthfully, she wasn't holding her breath on that one. These days, any killer who watched true-crime documentaries, or even scripted procedurals, would likely leave with the murder weapon to avoid being tracked down through DNA or fingerprints tying them to the crime. There were always exceptions, of course, with those who were overconfident or not privy to modern-day police work.

Garrett scratched his chin. "What about the victim's personal belongings?"

"The key to her car was still in her pocket and collected as evidence," Madison pointed out. "But Olivia's cell phone, along with her driver's license, is apparently missing. As for other belongings, given that she appeared to be on the parkway for a run, she probably kept her wallet or handbag hidden in her car. That isn't to say Olivia didn't have cash on her when she started out. If so, it's missing now."

He seemed to make a mental note before saying, "We can assume that the unsub may have taken the cell phone and anything else of immediate value."

Madison lifted a brow. "You think this was a robbery gone horribly wrong?"

"Quite the contrary. The apparent viciousness of the attack tells me that it was personal. Or something to that effect. Taking her possessions, if any, was strictly after the fact."

This made sense to her, though Madison was unaware of any clear-cut enemies Olivia had. Though she had recently ended a relationship, it had appeared as though it had been mutual and without malice either way.

Much like how we parted ways, Madison thought.

"We'll be reaching out to the public for any photographs or videos that may have been taken this morning in and around the area," she said, "to assist in our investigation. Or if anything or anyone suspicious was seen during the livestream of the Blue Ridge Parkway's webcams."

"Good." Garrett nodded. "Let's see what comes up."

Madison sighed. "Whoever did this was brazen and is obviously very dangerous while still on the loose."

"Tell me about it."

He frowned, closing his eyes for a moment, and

she sensed that Garrett might have been thinking about the stabbing death of his own mother on this very parkway some thirty years ago in what had turned out to be an unsolved homicide. Madison knew he had a chip on his shoulder because of it. Even going so far as to believe that, at five years of age, he might have been able to thwart the deadly attack had he only been present. Would these painful reminiscences hamper his ability to conduct this investigation?

"Do you know if the victim has any relatives in the area?" he asked, bringing Madison back to the present.

"Her dad lives in Kiki's Ridge," she said. "Not far from where Olivia stayed."

"I need to go see him." Garrett's voice was equable. "Apart from notifying the next of kin and you identifying the victim, we still need a family member for formal identification of her."

"I know." Madison understood how things worked from both her own experience as a law enforcement ranger and her siblings in the business who were also called upon to be the bearer of bad news from time to time. "I'd like to be there when you tell her dad, Steven Forlani. I owe Olivia that much as her friend and neighbor."

"Of course." He gazed at her. "This is your case as much as it is mine. We'll do this together."

"Thank you." She welcomed his cooperation and understanding. Moreover, she liked the notion of them working together on a case. Even if they had failed at working things out romantically.

Madison received word on her radio that a vehicle registered to Olivia Forlani had been located in a Blue Ridge Parkway Visitor Center parking lot. "We're on our way," she told dispatch.

"Maybe the car can tell us something," Garrett speculated.

"Maybe," she agreed, but she suspected that the attacker had not followed Olivia from her vehicle. Instead, it seemed more likely that the unsub had either been lying in wait for her off the trail or had come upon Olivia randomly, while still targeting her for the kill.

When they reached the parking lot, Madison recognized her friend's white Toyota Camry.

"It was undisturbed and all by its lonesome," Nicole Wallenberg, a park ranger, reported.

Madison examined the vehicle. There were no indications that something was amiss. It was locked, and nothing seemed unusual inside at first glance. She spotted an item of clothing on the back seat that appeared to be concealing something beneath it, such as Olivia's handbag.

She gazed at the twentysomething ranger, with a tousled dark bob parted on the side and blue eyes, and asked her to be sure, "You saw no one checking out the vehicle?"

"Nope."

Another park ranger, Leonard Martin, joined them. African American, tall, solid in build and in his thirties, with curly dark hair beneath his campaign hat and wearing shades, he backed Nicole up. "I took a look around and didn't see anyone who was acting suspicious."

"Why don't you see if the ranger in the visitor center can tell us if Ms. Forlani ever went inside," Garrett told them. "And if she had company or there was anyone who may have followed her."

Leonard nodded and Nicole said, "We'll check it out," before they walked off.

Madison took out her cell phone. "I'll try calling Olivia and make sure she didn't leave her phone inside the vehicle."

"Good idea," he said and looked in the car window. "Go ahead."

She made the call, and it rang through her end. Neither of them heard Olivia's phone coming from the car or otherwise gave any indication that it was in the car.

"It's not there," Madison surmised, which told her that, short of the phone being located by investigators, there was a good chance that it was in the possession of the unsub.

"We'll ping her number and see if we can pinpoint the cell phone's location."

She nodded. "Let's hope it's being used or was left on."

"In the meantime, Forensics can see if they can come up with anything material to the investigation when they go through the car," Garrett said.

"Given that her car key wasn't taken, I'm thinking

that the unsub never had any interest in stealing the vehicle," she said.

"I think you're right." He studied the vehicle again. "Whoever murdered your friend, he or she had another agenda than auto theft."

Madison squirmed at the thought of who might have wanted Olivia dead. "We need to know exactly what that was."

He nodded. "First, the victim's next of kin needs to know what happened to her."

"Right." She gulped, dreading what had to be done.

GARRETT WAS ADMITTEDLY finding it hard to keep his concentration on the road as he drove down Highway 18 South with Madison alongside. He vividly remembered when they'd been all over each other before everything had fallen apart. Now they were simply supposed to forget their history and focus on what, the present investigation and nothing else?

"So, how have you been?" he asked, hoping it didn't come across as awkward as it sounded to him.

"I've been good," she responded coolly, without looking directly at him. "How about you?"

"Same. Just work and more work." He wondered if she was seeing anyone. Though he had gone on a date every now and then, the truth was she was a hard act to follow for any other woman.

Madison batted her eyes wryly. "Not even a little play?"

Garrett chuckled. Was this a test to see if he was sleeping around? "Only when I forced myself to step away from the demands of the job," he told her. "Maybe a little hiking, working out or whatever distractions came my way." *Did I just give her the wrong message?* he asked himself, though not exactly sure what that was.

"I see," she muttered thoughtfully. "Thank goodness for those distractions that life can offer."

"It's not what you think," he spoke defensively.

"Not thinking anything," Madison insisted. "What you do and who you do it with these days is your own business."

"True enough." He couldn't argue with the philosophy of her tart statement. Which was just as true in reverse. Their relationship had ended before he'd left. They weren't dating any longer. Therefore they didn't owe the other any explanations on their love lives. Or lack thereof. So why did he feel the need to clarify where things stood with him in that department? While also wondering what lucky guy, if any, had taken his place in her life.

"I am curious, though, about how you ended up back in the South Atlantic-Gulf Region," she said. "What, did they kick you out of the Southwest Region? Or maybe you grew homesick?"

Garrett was struck by the bluntness of her inquiries. Sounded like she'd missed him. Or was that more wishful thinking? "Well, I was actually making a real impact with the field office in the Grand Canyon," he responded confidently. Never mind the fact that maybe he had been a bit hasty in his departure from North Carolina. If he could backtrack, things might have gone a different way between them.

"So, what happened?" Her voice crooned with impatience.

"What happened is that Special Agent Robin Grayson unexpectedly retired and, since they were already short on qualified agents with my experience, I was brought back to this region to take her place." He wrinkled his brow. "Not like I had much of a choice."

"And if you had?" Madison regarded him challengingly.

Sensing it was a backed-into-a-corner-type question, Garrett gave an answer that maybe even surprised himself a little. "I think it would have been the same result." Not sure how he wanted her to read that, he lightened the response by saying, "It gets too damned hot in Arizona, and the wasps and bees were a pain in the neck, no pun intended."

She laughed. "I'll bet."

Garrett liked the sound of her chuckle. She hadn't done it enough the first time around. Now seemed like it might be a wise time to change the subject again. "So, how's your family?"

"Everyone's doing great." She paused. "We got together earlier this summer for my sister's wedding and had lots of fun."

"Nice. Congrats to the newlyweds." A twinge of envy and regret rolled through him. It would have been nice to have tagged along. Even if their own romance had fizzled.

Garrett gazed at the road. If truthful about it,

when they'd been together, he had found himself slightly intimidated by Madison's family members, all in law enforcement professions. It had been almost as though he'd needed to prove himself. On the other hand, he felt more than up to the task of doing just that. Maybe the opportunity would present itself again.

"So, how long have you been friends with Olivia?"

She considered this. "Probably seven or eight months. Why?"

"Just wondering if there was anyone in her life who may have wanted her dead."

"She never said anything to me about being afraid of someone." Madison drew a breath. "Not that she would have necessarily, as not everyone is as comfortable talking about such things, sometimes believing it was something manageable. Till proven otherwise."

"What about a boyfriend?"

"Olivia had been seeing someone till about a month ago," Madison informed him. "A bank manager named Allen Webster. They supposedly ended things amicably, and I never heard her say anything about him being a problem after the fact."

"Hmm…" Garrett's voice was low, thoughtful. He understood that not all things were as they seemed. Especially when it came to dating and domestic violence and the ability of many to keep up appearances, for one reason or another. Was that the case here? "Do you know if she started seeing anyone else?"

"Olivia went out on dates every now and then, but she never indicated that anyone was stalking her."

"We'll see about that," he said, "assuming the investigation doesn't point in a different direction."

They reached Kiki's Ridge, and shortly thereafter he pulled up to a ranch style home on Ferris Lane. Parked in the driveway was a silver Ford Escape. "Someone's home."

"That's Steven Forlani's car," Madison noted.

Garrett took a breath. "Better deliver the bad news."

She nodded, and he could see that this would be difficult for her but knew she would handle it as a pro. Just as he would in having to deal with this part of their occupations.

THEY HEADED UP to the house and heard a dog barking inside. The door opened just as they stepped onto the porch. Olivia's father was in his midsixties and kept his head shaved bald. Madison could see the French bulldog in the backdrop, itching to come out but trained enough not to do so.

"Hi, Steven," she said, ill at ease.

"Madison," he acknowledged tentatively, turning his gray eyes upon Garrett.

"This is National Park Service Special Agent Sneed," she introduced.

Steven nodded at him. "Agent Sneed." He turned back to her.

"We need to talk to you about Olivia."

"What's happened?" he asked nervously.

"Can we talk inside?" Garrett spoke up.

Steven allowed them in and peered at Madison. "What's going on?"

She glanced at the dog, who was studying her with curiosity as he sat beside a leather recliner, and then at Garrett, before eyeing Olivia's father steadily. "I'm afraid I have bad news," she began. "There's no easy way to say this. Olivia's dead."

Steven's knees buckled. "What? How?"

"She was killed on the Blue Ridge Parkway."

"By who?" he demanded.

"That's still under investigation," Garrett told him. "I'm sorry for your loss."

Steven ran a hand across his mouth. "Why would someone do this?"

"We're trying to figure that out." Madison looked at him compassionately.

Garrett said, "Sir, we need you to come to the morgue to positively identify the body."

Olivia's father lowered his chin in agreement, and Madison knew that his pain would get worse before it got better, as was the case for all secondary victims dealing with homicides.

While they waited for him outside, she told Garrett, "You know, his only true peace will come when we catch the unsub. And even then…"

Nodding, he said thoughtfully, "Sometimes that peace never comes." He sighed, and she mused about the grief that was obviously still in his heart over his mother's tragic death. Something that Madison could relate to on a different level in losing her own parents in a car accident. "But we can't let that stop us from giving it our best shot, right?"

"Right." Madison knew that while the victimization of Garrett's mother had moved into the cold-case category that might never be resolved, Olivia's case was still very much open and solvable as they moved forward in the investigation.

Chapter Three

After her shift ended, Madison drove her duty car down the Blue Ridge Parkway and onto Highway 21 North before soon reaching the area where she lived in Kiki's Ridge. Nestled in the Blue Ridge Mountains, the quaint town had fewer than two thousand residents—most of whom knew or had heard of each other and would therefore be affected to some extent once the news spread about the murder of Olivia Forlani.

Turning onto Laurelyn Lane, Madison came upon her two-story, two-bedroom mountain chalet. She had purchased it three years ago and loved everything about it, including the creek out back, a great deck and easy access to walking trails and the river. The only thing missing was someone to share it with.

Having grown up in a large family, she was anything but a loner. But the one person she'd thought there might be a future with had just upped and left, putting that fantasy to bed. Now he was back, reminding Madison of what they'd once had, even when she fully expected Garrett to return to Atlanta when the current case was over.

Parking and going inside, she took in the place with its open concept, a floor-to-ceiling window wall with amazing views of the landscape, midcentury furnishings and hickory hardwood flooring. She headed up the winder stairs, removed her clothing and hopped into the shower of her en suite bathroom. Afterward, she wrapped her long hair in a towel and slipped into a more comfortable cotton camp shirt and jeans before heading back downstairs barefoot.

Madison went into the rustic kitchen, took a beer out of the stainless-steel fridge and went into the living room, where she grabbed her cell phone. Sitting on a retro button-tufted armchair, she called her sister, Annette, for a video chat to catch up.

After she accepted the request, Annette's attractive face came onto the screen. Biracial and a few years younger than Madison, her wavy brunette hair was long and parted in the middle with bangs that were chin length. Annette's brown-green eyes twinkled as she said, "Hey."

"Hey." She smiled back, while feeling envious that her sister had recently tied the knot with her dream guy and was experiencing the marital bliss that Madison could only dream of at this point.

"What's happening in the Blue Ridge Mountains these days?" Annette asked her.

"Since you asked, some bad and still-yet-to-be-determined things."

"Hmm… Why don't you start with the bad," her sister prompted.

"All right." Madison sat back. "A friend of mine was murdered today on the parkway."

"Oh, that's awful." Annette made a face. "I'm so sorry."

"Me too. Olivia was so full of life, and now that's been taken away from her."

"Do you have the killer in custody?"

"Not yet." Madison furrowed her brow. "It's still under investigation, but as long as the killer remains on the loose, it's not a good look for the National Park Service and park visitors in general, who want to feel it's a safe place to hang out."

"I'll bet. I'm sure you'll solve the case soon."

"Hope so."

Annette paused. "So, what's the still-yet-to-be-determined news?"

Madison took a sip of the beer and responded ambiguously, "You'll never guess who showed up from the NPS as the lead investigator in the case."

Her sister cocked a brow. "Garrett…?"

"Yeah." Madison was not at all surprised at her quick powers of deduction, given that Annette had held her proverbial hand when things had gone south between her and Garrett. "He was reassigned to this region and handed the case."

"How do you feel about that?"

"Truthfully, I'm still processing it," she answered.

"Maybe he is too," Annette threw out. "Have you had a chance to talk?"

"Not really, other than about the investigation and generalities."

"Well, my advice to you is just wait and see how things play out," Annette told her. "You never know, you two just might be meant for each other after all, bumps in the road notwithstanding."

Madison chuckled. "I wouldn't get too carried away with this," she said. "Things between us ended for a reason. There is no magic wand that will change that. We both have a job to do and will do it. No expectations. No pressures."

"Whatever you say." Annette smiled. "Just know that I have your back, wherever life takes you."

"Thanks, sis. I have yours too."

After ending the conversation, Madison heated up some leftover chicken casserole to go with a freshly made tossed salad, ate and thought about losing a friend and possibly regaining a friendship all in the same day.

THE NEXT MORNING, Madison drove to the headquarters of the Pisgah Ranger District on Highway 276 to update her supervisor, Law Enforcement Ranger Tom Hutchinson, on the investigation into Olivia's death. It was hardly an everyday occurrence on the Pisgah Region of the Blue Ridge Mountains but was something that needed to be dealt with in as expeditious a manner as possible.

When she arrived, Madison went directly into Tom's small office, cluttered with computer equipment and papers. He was sitting at a wooden desk, talking on his cell phone. In his late forties, thick-set, with thinning brown hair in a short, brushed back style and blue eyes, he was in uniform. Only a few months on the job, he had replaced the previous district ranger, Johnny Torres, who had been fired after getting arrested for soliciting an undercover cop whom he'd believed to be a sex worker.

Cutting his call short, Tom said, "Hey."

Madison said the same and then, "I wanted to drop by and talk about what happened on the park-way."

"Sit." He motioned toward a well-worn guest chair, which she took. "I'm sorry about your friend," he said sincerely. "There are no words to express how shocked I am."

"I feel the same," she told him, but she wanted to express her feelings anyway. "Olivia loved running in the park. That someone would go after her is un-conscionable."

"I agree." Tom sat back in his ergonomic office chair. "The fact this happened on my watch, and yours, makes it a priority that we work hand in hand with the special agent assigned to the case."

"I know." Madison gazed across the desk. "His name is Garrett Sneed. We've worked together be-fore." She saw no reason to mention their prior ro-mantic involvement, as that had ended two years ago and had no bearing on the current homicide in-vestigation.

"That's good," Tom said. "Should make it easier to

coordinate your efforts, along with other law enforcement, to solve this case."

"True." She had no problem working with Garrett, as he was obviously very good at his job, having been brought back to this region because of that. "I'll be sure to keep you updated on any developments along the way."

"Thanks, Madison." He smiled. "Let me know if there's anything you or Agent Sneed need in bringing this case to a close."

"I will."

After leaving the office, Madison drove to the Blue Ridge Parkway, wondering what Garrett was up to this morning. She pictured him starting the day with a workout of some sort before getting down to business. Apart from wanting to do his job successfully, she suspected that losing his mother in a similar manner had given Garrett even more motivation to solve Olivia's murder.

Madison's daydreaming was interrupted when she received a call over the radio from Nicole, who said, "I've got a potential witness regarding the murder who you may want to talk to."

Madison was attentive. "Who?"

"Maintenance Ranger Ward Wilcox."

After Nicole gave her the location, Madison said hurriedly, "I'm on my way." Before she passed this along to Garrett, she needed to see if the information was credible.

Upon going through a tunnel and farther into the Blue Ridge Mountains, driving alongside mountain ridges, she reached her destination. She parked and headed into a wooded area, not far from where Olivia's body had been found. Nicole and Leonard were standing there with Ward Wilcox.

Madison recognized him, having seen him around and spoken to him on occasion as a park employee. In his midsixties, Ward was tall and seemed in reasonably good shape for a man his age. He had dark eyes with heavy bags underneath on a weathered square face and wavy, gray locks in a shoulder-length bob. He wore a maintenance uniform and sturdy work shoes.

"Hey," Nicole said, wearing a campaign hat with her uniform.

"Hey." Madison glanced at the other ranger.

"Ward has something interesting to say," Leonard told her.

Madison gazed at the man. "Ward."

"Tell her what you told me," Nicole urged him.

"Okay." Ward sighed. "Yesterday, I saw a guy who was acting strange and holding on to a cell phone as if it contained the secrets to the universe. When I tried to talk to him, he ran off and disappeared into the woods."

"When was this?" Madison asked.

"I'd say around eight in the morning or so. Hadn't really given it much thought till I heard later about the young woman found dead on the parkway and started to put two and two together." Ward ran a hand through his hair. "Maybe it was nothing at all. Maybe it was something. Thought you needed to know, one way or the other."

"Glad you reported this," she told him, well aware that any possibilities in a murder case were worth pursuing, even if they led nowhere. She was curious, in particular, about the cell phone the man had been carrying. Olivia's phone was still missing and was believed to have been taken by the unsub. "Do you remember the color of the cell phone the man was holding?"

"Yeah," Ward said without prelude. "It was red."

Olivia's phone case was red, Madison told herself. Coincidence? The timeline for when Olivia might have been murdered fit too.

"You said this man was acting strange. How so?"

Ward scratched his chin. "I don't know. Just seemed like he was agitated. Something was definitely off about him."

"Can you describe him?" she asked intently.

"Yeah, I think so."

Madison listened as he gave the description of a slender, lanky, sandy-haired man with a scruffy beard in his early to midtwenties and wearing dirty jeans, a T-shirt that may have had something resembling blood on it and dark tennis shoes.

"What do you think?" Nicole pursed her lips in looking at Madison. "Could this be the killer?"

"Seems to fit," Leonard contended.

Though unwilling to take that leap, it was more than enough for Madison to look into the possibility seriously. "I think we need to find him and have a talk with him…and soon."

GARRETT WAS UP early in the two-bedroom log mountain cabin he had rented, located just off the Blue Ridge Parkway. It had contemporary furnishings, a full kitchen, Wi-Fi, white-oak hardwood floors, a private deck and enough space for him to operate. He had turned one of the bedrooms into his temporary office, using the oak table within as his desk. Admittedly, he hadn't slept very well, as Madison had been as much on his mind as the death of her friend. It was unfortunate that a homicide should bring them back together. At least in an investigative capacity. Though he wasn't necessarily opposed to rekindling what they'd had two years ago, Garrett doubted that Madison had much interest in going down memory lane. Could he blame her? What was done was done. No going back. Was there?

Having had a quick run on the property's hiking trail, he now sat in the small accent chair in front of his laptop, sipping on a mug of coffee, while reading the autopsy report on Olivia Forlani. According to the medical examiner, the victim had been stabbed eleven times in something akin to a horror movie, with deep stab wounds to the back, neck, shoulders and buttocks. Based on the injuries and patterns thereof, the still-missing murder weapon was described as likely a survival knife with a smooth eight-inch, single-edged blade. The cause of death was ruled a homicide, resulting from acute multiple sharp-force trauma inflicted upon the victim.

Garrett sucked in a deep breath, closing his eyes at the thought of the horrible death. He couldn't help but reminisce once again about the similar way that his mother's life had ended. Though he seriously doubted one had anything to do with the other, the two stabbing deaths still struck an eerie chord. Olivia Forlani's murder wouldn't go unpunished if he had any say in the matter.

His cell phone rang, and Garrett answered, "Sneed."

"Agent Sneed, this is Deputy Sheriff Pottenger."

Garrett recalled meeting Ray Pottenger of the Transylvania County Sheriff's Department yesterday when arriving at the Blue Ridge Parkway to take over the investigation. "Deputy," he said.

"Wanted to let you know that we pinged Olivia Forlani's cell phone and have tracked it to a campground not far from the parkway."

This told him that the unsub had turned on the phone and was likely using it. "Send me the info, and I'll get the ball rolling on a search warrant and meet you there."

"You've got it," Pottenger said.

After setting the wheels in motion for what he hoped would lead to Olivia's killer, Garrett phoned Madison to let her know what was going on. She answered after two rings. Before he could speak, she said, "There's a person of interest in Olivia's murder that you need to know about."

"Oh…" Garrett was all ears. "Go on."

"A maintenance ranger named Ward Wilcox reported seeing a man acting weird on the parkway yesterday at around the time Olivia may have been killed," Madison told him. "He was holding a cell phone that looked an awful lot like the one she owned. There may also have been blood on his T-shirt."

"Actually, I was calling you on that very subject," Garrett informed her, piqued by the news. "Deputy Sheriff Pottenger from the Transylvania County Sheriff's Department just phoned to say that Olivia's cell phone has been tracked to the Sparrow Campground on Bogue Lane."

"Really?" He could hear her voice perk up.

"Yeah. I'm on my way over there right now."

"I'll meet you there," she said eagerly.

"Okay." Garrett hoped they weren't in for a disappointment, knowing that this was personal for Madison. And if the truth be told, it was for him too. Her friend's death had managed to dredge up memories he would just as soon have kept buried. He was on his feet and got out the Glock 23 handgun he kept in a pistol case when not in use. Putting it in his shoulder holster, he headed out the door.

MADISON'S HEART WAS racing as she and the others approached the campsite. Her pistol was out and ready to use, if needed. She wanted to get a look at the unsub and possibly Olivia's killer. The fact that Ward Wilcox had seen what might have been her cell phone, coupled with it pinging in this location, seemed too much of a coincidence. When Garrett ordered the suspect out of the A-frame tent and there was no reply, deputies opened it. There was some clothing and other items for outdoor living haphazardly spread about. But no unsub.

Wearing latex gloves, Garrett went through the things in search of the cell phone. He came up empty but did pull out a T-shirt that appeared to have dried blood on it as well as what looked to be a hunting knife. "We need to get these analyzed and see if either has Olivia Forlani's DNA."

Deputy Sheriff Ray Pottenger, who was six-five and in his thirties with a dark crew cut beneath his campaign hat, gazed at him and said, "I'll get them straight over to the lab."

Madison took a peek inside the tent, and something caught her eye. "Looks like methamphetamine in the unsub's lair," she stated knowingly, "along with drug paraphernalia."

"I saw that," Garrett acknowledged. "Another reason to find out who this tent belongs to."

Putting away her gun, Madison got out her cell phone. "I'll try calling Olivia's number." She hoped that whoever had the phone and apparently cut it off before they could locate it had turned it back on.

To her surprise, she heard the phone ring. It was coming from the woods. She spotted a tall, slender man holding the phone. He promptly dropped it like it was a red-hot coal and bolted.

"Stop that man!" Madison's voice rose an octave. "He had Olivia's phone."

"We'll get him," Garrett promised, and they went after the unsub.

Following in pursuit, Madison took her gun back out while trying to keep pace. It didn't take long before they had the suspect cornered behind a beige Winnebago Revel RV. He was taken into custody without incident on suspicion of murder in the death of Olivia Forlani.

Chapter Four

The suspect was identified as Drew Mitchell. He was a twenty-six-year-old unemployed army vet, who'd served in Afghanistan before being discharged for misconduct. Garrett sat across from him in a wooden chair in an interrogation room at the Transylvania County Sheriff's Office in the city of Brevard on Public Safety Way. He gazed at the person of interest in Olivia Forlani's violent murder, while awaiting results from the DNA testing. Mitchell was around six feet tall, slender and blue eyed with dirty-blond hair in a long undercut and a messy beard. Apart from his current predicament, there was an outstanding warrant for Mitchell's arrest in South Carolina for burglary and drug possession.

"Why don't we just get right down to business," Garrett told him in no uncertain terms. "You're in a heap of trouble, Mr. Mitchell. But I'm sure you already know that."

"Okay, you got me." Mitchell's nostrils flared. "Yeah, busted for being an addict and stealing drugs. That's what happens when you run out of options."

"We're talking about more than drug addiction and possession." Garrett peered at him as he slid the cell phone that was inside an evidence bag across the table. "Care to tell me about this?" The suspect remained mute. "It belongs to a woman named Olivia Forlani. She was stabbed to death yesterday. Have anything to say about that?"

Mitchell squirmed. "I didn't kill anyone," he spat defiantly. "I swear."

Garrett rolled his eyes doubtingly. "You want to explain how you were caught with the victim's cell phone?"

"I found it." His voice thickened. "The phone was lying near some bushes. I needed a cell phone, so I took it. I had no idea the person the phone belonged to was dead."

"Is that why you ran when we came looking for you in your tent?" Garrett wasn't sure he was buying this. "Or why you took off when the maintenance ranger confronted you yesterday while you were in possession of the phone?"

"I ran when you guys showed up because I knew there was a warrant for my arrest. I freaked out." The suspect sucked in a deep breath. "I ran away when the maintenance dude came up to me because I thought he might try to take away the cell phone. I didn't want to give it up. So I fled."

Garrett remained less than convinced he was on the level and glanced up at the camera, knowing that Madison and other law enforcement were watching the live video. "Why was there blood on the T-shirt you wore yesterday?" he asked pointedly.

"I cut myself," Mitchell said tersely.

"What were you doing with a hunting knife inside the tent?" Garrett pressed the suspect. "Did you use it to cut someone?" Even in asking, in his mind, it didn't appear to be the same knife described in the autopsy report as the murder weapon in Olivia Forlani's death.

"I only used the knife for gutting an animal and have it for defending myself," Mitchell insisted. "I never cut anyone with it!"

Garrett went back and forth with him for a few more minutes, in which the suspect stuck to his story of innocence in the murder of Madison's friend. When they were interrupted by Deputy Pottenger, Garrett stood and walked over to the door.

"What do you have for me?" he asked him.

Pottenger sighed. "The tests on the T-shirt and knife have come back. It's Mitchell's blood on the T-shirt," the deputy said. "Blood found on the hunting knife came from an animal."

Garrett frowned. "So, no DNA found belonging to the victim?"

"Not as yet." Pottenger glanced at the suspect. "I think he's telling the truth about finding the cell phone."

Even though he wanted to believe otherwise, Garrett was inclined to side with the deputy. Drew Mitchell was going down on drug and theft charges—but apparently was not the killer of Olivia Forlani.

WITH DREW MITCHELL seemingly no longer the lead suspect in Olivia's death, it seemed logical to Madison that they go back to square one in the investigation. That meant interviewing the last known person Olivia had been involved with—Allen Webster. Though there were no obvious red flags to believe he'd had anything to do with her death, he needed to be checked out. Between her own years in law enforcement and stories she'd heard from her siblings and parents, Madison knew that a high percentage of female victims of homicides were killed by current or former significant others. Could that have happened in this instance?

I'll withhold judgment till we speak to Allen, Madison told herself as she drove with Garrett to Kiki's Ridge Bank on Vadon Street, where Allen Webster was the manager.

"Mitchell could have still killed Olivia and gotten rid of the murder weapon," Garrett suggested, behind the steering wheel.

Madison turned to his profile. "You really think so?"

"It's possible, though unlikely." He pulled into the bank's parking lot. "We have to keep all suspects on the table, so to speak. But as for now, Mitchell seems too messed up and sloppy to have pulled this off without a hitch."

"You're probably right," she agreed musingly. "We'll see what Olivia's ex has to say."

"Yeah." Garrett turned to her. "You okay?"

She met his eyes. "I'm fine. Like you, I just want answers, you know?"

"I do." He touched her hand, and she got a surprising jolt, as if struck by lightning. "We'll find them, wherever we need to look."

Madison nodded, feeling reassured somehow by his strength in words and conviction, along with the gentleness of his touch. They left the car and headed inside the bank. After Garrett flashed his identification to a burly and bald security guard, they made their way to Allen Webster's office. Sitting at a U-shaped desk, Madison recognized the man from a time she'd gone out for drinks with Olivia and him. In his late thirties and wearing a navy suit, Allen was muscular and gray-eyed with dark hair in a short fade.

"National Park Service Special Agent Sneed," Garrett told him.

"Agent Sneed." Allen shifted his gaze and said, "Madison…er, Ranger Lynley… I guess you're here to talk to me about Olivia?"

"That's correct." Garrett eyed him. "We need to ask you a few questions."

"Of course. Please sit." He proffered a long arm at the designer guest chairs in front of his desk, which they took. "I'm still trying to wrap my head around what happened to Olivia. Not sure how I can be of any help, but I'll do my best."

"Thank you," Madison said politely. "We're just covering the bases as we try to find out who killed her."

"I understand," he said evenly. "Olivia and I

stopped seeing each other a few weeks ago. I have no knowledge about who might have murdered her. If there was something else you needed—"

"You can start off by telling us where you were yesterday between, say, seven and ten in the morning," Garrett said.

"Right here." Allen quickly lifted his cell phone and studied it. "Just wanted to take a look at my schedule to pinpoint exactly what was going on then." He paused. "Had a staff meeting to start the morning and then made a few phone calls and did some work on my laptop. All of this can be easily verified."

Madison had no reason to doubt that he was telling the truth, though they would check out his alibi. Still, she asked, "So why did you and Olivia break up anyway?"

Allen sat back with a frown on his face. "We stopped clicking, to put it bluntly. It just seemed like we were spinning our wheels trying to make it work, till deciding mutually that we were better off as friends. I certainly never wanted anything like this to happen to her."

Neither did I, Madison thought sadly, while also relating to the reality that some lovers were better off as friends. She wondered if that was true with her and Garrett. "Do you know if there was anyone who might have wanted to harm Olivia?" she asked Allen.

He chewed on this for a moment, then responded, "Not really. But if you asked me if there was anyone who might benefit from her death, I'd have to say the person who was Olivia's chief competitor at the law firm where she worked—Pauline Vasquez. They had both been trying to make partner, and someone would be left out in the cold, so to speak. I'm not suggesting in any way that Pauline would have gone so far as to kill for the job. That's for you to determine."

"We'll look into it," Garrett said.

"Hope you solve this case." Allen took a breath. "Our differences aside, Olivia was really a good person and she deserves some justice."

"I agree." Madison met his eyes. "We'll do our best to see that she gets it."

They stood, along with Allen, who walked with them and introduced them to other employees, who verified his presence the previous morning, seemingly eliminating him as a suspect.

"What are your thoughts on the so-called rivalry between Olivia and Pauline Vasquez?" Garrett asked as he drove away from the bank.

"I'd heard Olivia mention it from time to time but saw it as a spirited but friendly competition, more or less, to make partner at the firm," Madison admitted. "But who's to say it didn't go much further than that? Women are just as capable of committing acts of violence as men, even if there's a lower incidence of it in society. It wouldn't be the first time that jealousy and fierce competition led to murder."

"True. Or the last. The law firm's not far from here," he pointed out. "We might as well swing by and see how Vasquez reacts."

"We should." She was in total agreement. "All possibilities remain open at this point, right?"

"Right. I have to say, though, that after reading the autopsy report, the viciousness of the attack has me believing the culprit is more likely than not a male."

"We'll see about that," she said, glancing at him.

Garrett kept an open mind. The fact that the case against Drew Mitchell fell through meant that the hunt for Olivia's killer was wide open and the potential suspects were not gender specific.

They reached the Kiki Place Office Building on Twelfth Street and Bentmoore. After parking in an underground garage, they took the elevator up to the third-floor law offices of Eugenio, Debicki and Vasquez.

"Why don't you interview Ms. Vasquez," Garrett told Madison as they stepped inside the lobby. "I'll check out the rest of the firm and see if anyone might have had it in for Olivia."

"All right," she agreed, and they approached a reception desk.

MADISON ENTERED THE carpeted office of Pauline Vasquez, the newest partner in the law firm. *She didn't waste any time*, Madison thought as she was greeted by Olivia's former colleague. In her thirties, Pauline was small and attractive with long brunette feathered hair and green eyes. She wore a brown skirt suit and high heels.

"Law Enforcement Ranger Madison Lynley," she introduced herself.

"Pauline Vasquez." She offered her hand, and Madison shook it. "All of us here have taken Olivia's death very hard. She was a valued employee."

"And one you no longer have to worry about beating you out for partner," Madison said in pulling no punches.

Pauline expressed disapproval. "If you're suggesting that I had something to do with Olivia's death…"

"Did you?" Madison questioned sharply to see if this shook her up any. "You apparently had the most to gain by her death."

"I had nothing to do with that," she insisted, running a hand liberally through her hair. "Yes, we were both battling to make partner, however, I was actually given the news that I'd been the one chosen several days ago, but was told to keep it under wraps till the official announcement, which coincided with Olivia's tragedy." Pauline sighed. "In any event, I would not have resorted to murdering my rival for the privilege. I achieved this on my own merits as a hard worker. Nothing more."

Madison held her gaze. "In that case, I'm sure you have a rock-solid alibi for where you were yesterday morning between seven and eleven?"

Pauline sighed exaggeratedly. "As a matter of fact, I do. I was in Raleigh, doing work for the firm. I arrived the night before and returned to Kiki's Ridge last night after eight o'clock. You can check the flights, the hotel I stayed at, two restaurants I went to and, of course, the meetings I attended."

"I'll do that." Madison took down her information

to that effect. As it was, she sensed that they were climbing up the wrong beanstalk with Pauline as Olivia's killer. Should it be proven that she had hired someone else to do her dirty work, that would come out sooner or later.

She forced a smile at the attorney. "Thanks for your time. I'll show myself out."

GARRETT STOOD BY a floor-to-ceiling window in the office of Henry Eugenio, the fiftysomething CEO of the law firm. Henry, who was slender and wearing a designer suit, with wavy gray hair in a side-swept style, expressed remorse about the murder of Olivia Forlani. This seemed genuine enough to Garrett. As did the support for Pauline Vasquez, whom he insisted had been chosen to make partner before Olivia's untimely death and, as such, would not have had any reason to harm her.

This only fed into Garrett's belief that the unsub was a male perpetrator. "Did Olivia ever have any trouble with men in the firm?" he asked him.

Henry pushed the silver glasses up his long nose and blinked blue eyes. "Not that I knew of. Everyone got along great with her."

No one gets along perfectly with everyone, Garrett thought. "So, you never heard anything about unwanted advances or anything like that?"

Pausing, Henry gazed out the window and back. "I was once told that one of our newer junior associates made a pass at Olivia," he said. "But as we strongly discourage office romances, that was put to rest pretty quickly. Olivia never indicated it went any further than that."

But what if it had and escalated into something more ominous than nonviolent sexual harassment? Garrett asked himself. "I'd like to question this junior associate, if I can."

"No problem," Henry responded. "I'll buzz him to come in."

"Actually, if it's all the same to you, I'd rather speak with him alone," Garrett said, not wanting the suspect to be unnerved by an interrogation in front of his boss, perhaps causing him to lie.

"Whatever you say, Agent Sneed."

"What's his name?"

"Alex Halstead."

"Just point me in the right direction, and I'll find him," Garrett said after Henry had walked him out of the office.

"All right," he agreed, touching his glasses. "I'm sure you'll find that Alex was not involved in Olivia's death."

Garrett knew there was a tendency to see the best in people. Till proven otherwise. "Hope you're right about that."

A few doors down, he saw the nameplate and went into the office. In his late twenties, tall and fit, Alex was blue-eyed and had dark hair in a French crop style. He was standing and approached Garrett.

"Alex Halstead?"

"Yeah?" He tilted his face. "Did we have a meeting scheduled?"

"No," Garrett responded, realizing the man had him by two inches. "I'm Special Agent Sneed from the Investigative Services Branch of the National Park Service. I'm investigating the murder of Olivia Forlani."

Alex wrinkled his nose. "Sorry to hear about Olivia," he claimed. "She was a great lawyer." He paused. "What do you need from me?"

"I understand that you hit on her," Garrett said, peering suspiciously.

"Yeah. It was a mistake."

"Some people don't know how to take no for an answer," Garrett stated.

"Not me," Alex insisted. "I apologized and never went there again."

"Can you account for your whereabouts yesterday morning?"

"I was at my apartment, sleeping through a hangover after getting wasted the night before," he responded quickly. "Didn't get up till noon. It was my day off."

Garrett eyed him. "Can anyone verify this?"

Alex cocked a brow. "If you're asking if I was with someone, the answer is no." He frowned. "If you're implying that I went after Olivia on the parkway because she didn't go out with me, you're way off base. I may not be perfect, but I'm definitely not a killer."

Aware that not all alibis included witnesses, Garrett was left to give him the benefit of the doubt, in the absence of evidence to the contrary. "I'll take your word for that."

"Thanks," he said smugly.

"By the way, you don't happen to own a survival knife, do you?" Garrett thought he would throw that out there, considering that the murder weapon was still unaccounted for.

Alex narrowed his eyes. "I'm not a hunter, outdoorsman, survivalist or anything like that," he contended. "So that would be no."

"Then I guess that will be all for now," Garrett told him. "If anything else comes up, I know where to find you."

He left the office, believing that Alex Halstead had not killed Olivia Forlani.

Chapter Five

"Do you want to grab a bite to eat?" Madison asked Garrett during the drive, after they had compared notes on Pauline Vasquez and Alex Halstead. Neither seemed likely as Olivia's killer, joining Drew Mitchell as former suspects as things stood. That meant they still had their work cut out for them if they were to catch the perpetrator before the case could start to run cold.

"I'm down with that," Garrett told her. "Actually, I'm starved."

For some reason, Madison felt relieved, as though she'd feared he would decline the dinner invite, which she'd only made because she too was hungry. Since they were still out, it seemed like a good idea, with no expectations beyond a good meal.

"I thought we could go to Janner's Steakhouse," she suggested, given that it was just around the corner. Never mind the fact that it had been a favorite place for them to dine when they'd been dating.

He smiled. "Sounds good."

Soon they were seated at a table by the window,

where Madison ordered a boneless ribeye steak and heirloom tomato salad, then watched as Garrett went with familiar lamb chops and au gratin potatoes. *Apparently some things never change*, she thought, amused. They both chose a glass of Cabernet Sauvignon wine to sip on.

"So, what's next in the search for a killer?" Madison asked as a relatively comfortable conversation starter while she tasted the wine.

Garrett considered this. "Well, we need to go back over everything we have and don't have, including going through Olivia's belongings with the cooperation of her father, and see what we can gauge from this in deciphering possible clues on the unsub."

"I get that, but what do you think drove the perp into attacking Olivia in particular?" she posed to him curiously as the chief investigator. "Since it doesn't appear as yet that she was being stalked."

"That's the thing," he said, sitting back. "We don't know that is the case. Yes, it could well have been a random attack. But if Olivia was a regular jogger on the parkway, the unsub may have been aware of this pattern and waited for just the right time to strike."

Madison cringed. "Olivia and I liked to jog together sometimes on trails in the Pisgah Region," she noted. "Not to mention my own solo runs. Her killer could have been spying on me as well."

"That's always a possibility." Garrett furrowed his brow. "Did you ever see anyone who aroused your suspicions?"

"I honestly can't say that was the case," she replied contemplatively. "On the other hand, I always try to be on guard for any human or wildlife threats, but it's quite possible that an unassuming predator could have escaped my notice."

"Well, do me a favor—let's not have any more solo runs for the time being until we catch this person. I'd hate for you to be faced with the threat of a knife-wielding killer."

"All right." She felt that his concern for her safety was as much for what they'd had as his being a special agent. Not that she would have expected anything less, as his safety on and off the job was important to her too. "I won't make myself an easy target." Carrying her firearm when off duty, even for a run, was never a guarantee of safety these days. Especially if an assailant was armed too.

"Good." Garrett tasted his wine. "Of course, if you need a temporary running mate, I'm happy to volunteer for the job. Just let me know."

"I will." Madison had not forgotten that he ran too and that they had enjoyed jogging and hiking together. She wondered if doing so would be so simple, if he had no intention of sticking around just as she started to grow comfortable with him again.

GARRETT FELT QUEASY at the thought that Olivia's killer could have had Madison in his sights. As a male assailant was the most likely unsub at this moment in time, Garrett was going on that assumption in their search for the culprit. Though there was no reason to believe as yet that Madison was being targeted, he was glad to know she would not make herself an easy mark for anyone. Of course, as an active member of law enforcement for the NPS and with family in this line of work, he had no doubt she could handle herself in almost any situation. But that didn't stop him from being concerned for her safety. Especially as long as he was around to help keep an eye on her, and her seeming willingness to allow him to do so.

When the food arrived and they began eating, Garrett felt the urge to see where things stood in Madison's love life at the moment. He studied her as she ate, finding himself turned on even with this normal act. She was once again in uniform as a ranger and still kept that hair in a bun. Neither stopped him from appreciating what was right in front of him. "So, are you seeing anyone these days?"

Madison looked up as though startled by what seemed to him a reasonable question. She stopped eating and responded succinctly, "No, I'm not."

He tried to read into that. Was this because she had just broken up with someone? Had she been single since their own relationship ended? Or was she not interested in dating anyone right now? "Any decent prospects?"

She laughed. "No—not even any indecent ones."

He grinned crookedly while slicing into a lamb chop. "Has there been anyone in your life since we broke up? Or is that none of my business?"

"No, and yes," she told him. She forked a piece of steak. "To be honest, I haven't been asked out by anyone who captured my fancy enough. But that could change." Madison rested her gaze upon him. "As for it being your business, you gave up that right when you moved across the country."

"Fair enough," he conceded, even when it had seemed best at the time. "Sorry for getting into your business. My bad."

"What about you?" Madison asked. "My turn to be bad. Who are you dating right now?"

"Not a soul." Garrett held her gaze. "Tried dating once in a while but, truthfully, it's been hard to get you out of my system. Not to say I've ever wanted to, even if we went our separate ways."

"Why did we anyway?" she posed in a casual manner.

"Excuse me?" He wasn't sure what she was getting at.

"Why did we go our separate ways?" Madison squared her shoulders. "I mean, it seemed like we had a good thing going. Then, just like that, it all went away." She sighed. "Or you did."

Garrett set down his scoop of au gratin potatoes. "As I recall, we both decided it was best that we end things between us. Or am I living in an alternate reality or something?" He regarded her questioningly, wondering if he somehow had it all wrong.

She took a deep breath. "You're not. It was what we both wanted. At least I thought so at the time. But we never really talked about this the way we probably should have. It was like burying our heads in the sand was easier than seeing if what we had was worth holding on to."

"I agree." He drank some water and grabbed his fork again reflectively. "It just seemed like neither of us was ready for a commitment, for whatever reasons. Maybe we were just trying to shield ourselves from being hurt. Or maybe the maturity or confidence level wasn't there to take that step in our relationship."

"We should have tried harder to see if there was more there." Madison pouted, while playing with her food. "I mean, didn't we owe ourselves that much? Or is it only me who can see that?"

"It's not just you." Garrett wasn't going to shy away from being equally culpable for their breakup. "I regret that we didn't hash through things more. Whatever we were running away from, we should have stopped and laid it all out and let the chips fall where they may. For better or worse."

Her mouth hung open. "You think?"

"Yeah," he admitted. "In hindsight, I wish I had stayed and worked harder to see where we went wrong. Or steered off course. But given the state of things, I thought that if I had stayed, it might be too weird being around each other and trying not to step on the other's toes while doing our jobs."

"You're right," she told him. "Probably would've been weird. Even if I wish we had done things differently."

"Me too." Garrett sat back, wondering where they went from here. Was there any chance at all for a redo? Was she open to this? Was he? "I never wanted us to stop being friends," he spoke truthfully. "But when I never heard from you again via text message, calls or whatever, I just assumed you had moved on and wanted no part of me in your life anymore."

Madison arched a thin brow. "I never meant for us to lose communication," she said in a heartfelt tone. "I wanted us to stay connected in some way. But after you left, I wasn't sure you felt the same way and didn't want to press it."

He nodded understandingly. "I did feel the same way," he promised her. "And didn't reach out to you more for the same reasons."

She smiled. "Looks like our communication skills really suck."

Garrett chuckled. "Yeah, probably could use some work."

"So, now that you're back in this region, can we at least be friends again?" Madison put forth hopefully. "We probably owe ourselves that much, regardless of how things ended between us."

In his mind, the *at least* part implied she might've been open to going beyond the friendship level. He felt that way too. Or at least exploring the possibilities. "Yes, I would like that," he told her.

She flashed him a toothy grin. "Cool."

He smiled back, already believing they had turned a corner and that the door was wide open for whatever might come next, over and beyond the investigation into Olivia Forlani's murder.

WHEN SHE GOT home that night, Madison was still thinking about the unexpected "airing things out" with Garrett. *It was overdue*, she told herself. She was unsure exactly what it meant in terms of going forward. Both had admitted to mistakes in the way they'd handled the situation two years ago. She wished they could go back and make things right. But there was no such thing as time travel, except in sci-fi, so they could only take what was handed to them and see what they wanted to do with it. They had agreed that a renewed friendship was a great place to start. Would it really be that simple though? Could either of them forget about what they'd once had and not want to have it again once the comfort level had kicked in?

Madison showered, brushed her teeth and went to bed. It was a country-style bed, like the other furnishings in the spacious room, and reminded her that it was where she and Garrett had first made love. A flicker of desire caused her temperature to rise before she brought it back down. She realized that in spite of the sexual chemistry that still existed between them, any attempts at recreating the passions they'd shared might do more harm than good. Even if he planned to stick around once the investigation had run its course, Atlanta, where Garrett lived, was still hours away. Did it really make sense to want to jump into what amounted to a long-distance relationship that could just as easily fizzle like the last time around?

Before an answer could pop into her head, Madison fell asleep. In her dreams, thoughts shifted to Olivia and the terrible way she died, along with needing to bring the killer to justice. No matter what it took.

OLIVIA FORLANI'S KILLER walked deep in the forest, surrounded by hemlock, hickory, birch and white pine trees. He was pensive as he approached Julian Price Lake along the Blue Ridge Parkway. The moon was starting to set beyond Grandfather Mountain, reflecting on the water's surface. He listened to the hoot of an eastern screech owl, then heard the crunch of his own cap-toe ankle boots on the dirt path. He was tempted to stop and take in his surroundings while breathing in the night air. But he forged on instead, eager to return to his campsite.

He thought about the one he had stabbed to death two days ago. It was something he had been thinking about for a long time, and when the opportunity had come his way, he hadn't hesitated to take it. Well, maybe he had paused for consideration, knowing that once he'd moved ahead, there would be no turning back. But the urge in him had been much too great to have second thoughts. Not when he had contemplated this moment in his head time and time again. But something had held him back, as if a voice from the grave was warning him against proceeding.

He'd suddenly become deaf to this as another voice had prodded him to continue what he had started long ago. This mighty call to kill had overtaken him the way illicitly manufactured fentanyl might get an addict in its grip.

So when Olivia Forlani had gone for her predictable run, he'd lain in wait to strike. And he had, over and over again. Till her blood-curdling screams had been no more, silenced by death. Making his getaway had been tricky, as others on the parkway could have spotted him and notified the authorities. But he was too smart to be caught, blending in as he had learned to do so well in his life. He had succeeded in taking away a life and rejuvenating his own in the process.

As he reached the campsite and the tent he called home these days, he could only crack a smile at the thought of his hiding from pursuers in plain view. Just as rewarding were the dark musings in his head that told him that the adrenaline rush he experienced in his homicidal urges was bound to come back again. Sooner than later. When that happened, he would find another to take the place of Olivia Forlani, in feeling the cold steel of his knife as he plunged it inside of her till death came mercifully.

He laughed in admitting that he was showing no mercy in his acts of violence. But then, none had been shown to him when he'd needed it most. Life worked out that way sometimes. He accepted this and wanted no sympathy. Nor would he give any.

Another wicked laugh escaped his lips, even as another call of an owl rang out, letting him know he was in preferable company as he retired for the night.

Chapter Six

The outdoor funeral service for Olivia Forlani was held at the Kiki's Ridge Cemetery. Garrett stood beside Madison to pay his respects to her friend. The fact that they had yet to make an arrest in her death bothered him. Someone was still out there, perhaps overconfident in the ability to avoid detection and apprehension. As he glanced at Olivia's father, Garrett couldn't help but think about his own mother and how the five-year-old version of himself had been overwrought at the notion that he would never see her again. Now Steven Forlani was in the same boat, more or less. The fact that he had gotten to see his daughter reach adulthood and achieve some of her professional objectives didn't make the pain of losing her prematurely to senseless violence any less.

Garrett gazed at Madison, remembering that she, too, had known such loss with the tragic death of her parents. No matter the manner of death, it was still a shock to the system and was something that would always be with you, whatever your lot in life.

"You okay?" he whispered to her.

Madison nodded. "Olivia's in a better place," she surmised.

"Yeah." Garrett wanted to believe this too for her friend, their parents and everyone who had moved on from this world.

He scanned the other mourners, seeing Olivia's colleagues huddled together. They seemed genuinely moved, and he wanted to believe none of them had anything to do with her death. Garrett eyed others in attendance, while wondering if Olivia's killer could be among them. As sick as it was, he was aware that some killers liked to come to funerals to gloat about their kills under the cloak of grievers. Was that the case here?

Garrett pondered this as he listened to the pastor sing the praises for Olivia, even as the perpetrator remained at large and the Blue Ridge Parkway a danger zone as a consequence. Till an unsub was made to answer for the homicide.

TWO DAYS LATER, Madison was on duty, patrolling the parkway. Garrett was still investigating Olivia's death, but no arrests had been made thus far. Madison was certain that it was only a matter of time before the unsub was behind bars. As she well knew, these type cases were not always cut and dried. The perp could have gone after Olivia for any number of reasons and now be as far away as Timbuktu in an effort to escape justice.

Well, you can run, but you can't hide, she thought. At least not forever.

Her musings turned to Garrett. They had resumed a friendship, which she liked, while also seemingly gone out of their way to smother any flames that could erupt into something more, as though a bad thing. Was it really? Or should they let it happen and deal with whatever came after?

Madison snapped out of the thoughts as she received a report over the radio that a black bear had been spotted on the parkway. And, worse, that it was threatening a young couple. Or was it the other way around? Black bears were, in fact, omnivores. They took up residence along the Blue Ridge Parkway and weren't afraid to venture out of their habitat in search of food. But sometimes curiosity and fascination got the better of visitors, who got too close to a bear, placing themselves in danger. Was that the situation here?

Either way, Madison was duty bound to come to their assistance. "I'm on my way," she told the dispatcher.

Shortly, she turned off US 221 at Milepost 294 and entered the parkway near Moses H. Cone Memorial Park and Bass Lake. Passing by a grassy hill, Madison spotted Leonard and Ward in a parking area. They were flagging her down, as though she couldn't see them.

When she pulled up to and exited her vehicle, Leonard said ill at ease, "The feisty black bear went after a couple just trying to enjoy their lunch."

"Where's the couple now?" Madison was concerned. "Were they harmed by the bear?"

"They're holed up in a Jeep Grand Cherokee Laredo over there," Ward said. "Apparently when the bear got aggressive, they were able to fend it off long enough to get into the SUV, with only a few scratches."

"Well, that's good anyhow," she told them. "Any sign of the bear?"

"As a matter of fact, it looks like we've got its attention." Leonard's voice shook. He angled his eyes toward the woods. "And it's scaring the hell out of me."

Madison saw that the black bear had reemerged and sized them up as potential prey, while snorting, popping its jaws and stomping its feet. With her heart skipping a beat, and not particularly interested in being the bear's meal, she raced back to her Tahoe and pulled out a 12-gauge shotgun. It was loaded with cracker shells which, when fired, would emit a loud booming sound in hopes of scaring off the animal.

As what looked to be a three-hundred-pound male took the measure of them while bellowing and standing on its hind legs, Madison ordered the two rangers to get behind her vehicle. Just as she was about to take cover too, the bear suddenly began to charge across the parking lot toward her. Tempted to panic but refusing to do so, she screamed at it and, remaining steady, placed the gun barrel at a forty-five-degree angle, firing the projectile in the bear's direction. It traveled some four hundred feet downrange before there was a flash and huge bang.

Repeating this seemed to do the trick as, spooked, the bear abruptly stopped in its tracks, pivoted and ran back off into the woods. Only then did Madison lower the shotgun and let out a deep breath. "Is everyone all right?" she asked, to be sure.

Leonard and Ward came out from behind the Tahoe. "We are now," Ward said. "Glad you showed up when you did, Ranger Lynley."

"Good shooting," Leonard quipped.

"You do what you have to do," she told them modestly, thankful things hadn't gotten out of control for her or the bear.

"You can come out now," Ward shouted to the young couple, still huddled inside their SUV. "I think the danger has passed."

Madison wasn't sure that the bear might not come back, when regaining his courage and desire for something to chow down on. She interviewed the couple, visiting from Hawaii, and could see that they were still shaken up from their ordeal. But otherwise not the worse for wear. Still, given the fact that the bear had attacked humans at all meant that rangers and wildlife biologists would need to locate it and act in accordance with the protocols of the North Carolina Wildlife Resources Commission.

With the present threat contained, Madison thought she might check out the woods close to the grassy area where the couple had been picnicking. She wanted to be sure that the black bear hadn't first gone after some other vacationers, who might be in trouble. The last thing she wanted was to see someone's dream turn into a nightmare, with no one the wiser till too late. Hopefully that bear had not caused more havoc to deal with.

Having walked along the trail and through the tall trees, with the sounds of nature all around her, Madison felt a sense of calm. She decided maybe all was well and she could get back in her patrol car. Later, she imagined that Garrett would probably tease her about the black-bear encounter. When something caught her periphery, Madison jerked her head in that direction. There was something lying between trees. Or someone.

Putting a hand to her mouth, she realized that it was Ranger Nicole Wallenberg who was lying flat on her back. At first glance, Madison thought that the black bear might have attacked her before going after the couple. But homing in on her fellow ranger, she believed otherwise.

Blood oozed from cuts through Nicole's uniform that appeared to have come from a knife. Her blue eyes were wide open but gave no signs of life.

Madison gulped. *It wasn't a bear attack*, she told herself. This wasn't the work of an animal but a homicide perpetrated by a human being. Much like that of Olivia. Someone was targeting women on the parkway.

GARRETT HELD MADISON as she rested her head on his shoulder. She wept a little over the murder of their colleague. Coming on the heels of Olivia's death, and apparently in the same manner, had undoubtedly shaken Madison. It grated on his nerves as well, as this told Garrett that they were likely looking at a serial killer who had chosen the Blue Ridge Parkway as the killing grounds.

Madison pulled away from him and uttered diffidently, "Sorry about that." She wiped her nose with the back of her hand. "Just kind of overwhelming that this would happen again."

"I know. And you don't have to apologize." Indeed, it felt quite natural to be comforting her, and he would happily do so anytime she needed this. "You have every right to feel unsettled with what happened."

"We both do," she pointed out. "Nicole was one of our own. Now she's dead."

"Yeah." Garrett turned to look at the dead ranger, lying just as Madison had found her. She had clearly been put through an ordeal before someone had taken her life. Who? Why had someone gone after the ranger? Did she have any connection with Olivia Forlani? Or were both women victims of opportunity?

The immediate area had been cordoned off, and the crime scene technicians and sheriff's deputies were processing it for evidence. Garrett contemplated the scenario: Madison had staved off a black-bear attack, preventing herself and others from being a good bear meal. This had been, in and of itself, an act of bravery on her part, even though it was part of the job description. Then a routine and necessary check of the perimeter and she'd come upon Nicole. Could Madison have scared the killer off? Or was this act of violence a pattern of behavior that had been well planned and executed before the unsub had made a getaway?

"So, you didn't see anyone?" Garrett asked evenly.

"No," Madison replied. "But I'd just left two rangers, and another ranger joined us. Haven't had the chance to question them as to whether or not anyone saw anything."

"Okay." He gazed at the dead ranger's body. "What about the couple who said they were attacked by the black bear?"

"They apparently left the parkway afterward, upset by the incident."

"Did either ranger actually witness their encounter with the bear?"

"I believe the rangers arrived after the fact." She looked up at him. "You think they might have something to do with Nicole's murder?"

"Probably not," Garrett answered, rubbing his jaw. "On the other hand, if they had, the bear roaming around would have been a convenient diversion. Then there is the timeline. Assuming Nicole was victimized around the same time, this would have given the couple a perfect means for distraction and escape. At the very least, they may have seen something while on the grassy hill. Or someone."

"Between webcams along the Blue Ridge Parkway and a good description of the vehicle driven by the couple," Madison said, "I'm pretty sure we can track them down."

"Good." Garrett turned to see that Dawn Dominguez had arrived to take over from here. "Dr. Dominguez," he acknowledged.

"Special Agent Sneed." Dawn looked to Madison. "Ranger Lynley."

Madison nodded. "The latest victim is a member of the National Park Service," she voiced sadly.

Dawn frowned. "So sorry about that." She glanced at Nicole. "I'll do my best to expedite matters in giving you what I can for your investigation."

"Thank you."

Garrett added, "We need to know how she died, signs of a struggle and approximately how long ago we're talking about when the incident occurred."

"Got it." Dawn met his eyes and slipped on nitrile gloves before immediately giving the decedent a preliminary examination.

After a few minutes, she told them, "From the looks of it, the victim was stabbed at least six times, maybe more. There does appear to be some defensive wounds, but no evidence thus far that she was able to get DNA from her attacker. No initial signs that this was a sexual assault."

"What about the time of death?" Garrett asked.

Dawn touched the decedent. "I'd say she was killed in the last hour or two."

Or in the same time span that the couple claimed they were attacked by a black bear, he thought. Looking at Madison, it was clear that she was thinking the same thing. They needed to find the pair, if only to eliminate them as suspects.

THIS WAS MADISON'S second time speaking on the phone with Tom since learning of Nicole Wallenberg's murder. Only this time it was on video chat and was no more of an easier pill to swallow than the first time. "The deputy medical examiner has more or less confirmed that Nicole was stabbed to death."

Tom's brow furrowed, and he muttered an expletive. "She had big dreams with the NPS," he said sourly. "They probably would have all come true."

"I think so too." Though Madison hadn't been that close to Nicole, they'd had the chance to speak on occasion outside of work. And the ranger had been enthusiastic in her job and where it might take her over a long career. Now any such plans had been put to rest.

"Where are things in the investigation?" Tom asked fixedly.

"We're interviewing anyone who may have information," she responded, knowing they had yet to locate the young couple who had been supposedly in fear of their lives from an aggressive black bear. Though she could attest to that much herself, Madison still had to consider them persons of interest in Nicole's death. Till they were ruled out.

"Do you and Special Agent Sneed believe this is related to the murder of Olivia Forlani?"

"It looks that way, at this point." Madison almost wished that weren't the case, hating to think that a serial killer was in their midst. But the similarities between the homicides couldn't be ignored. Including the fact that the murder weapon was yet to be found in either case.

Tom wrinkled his nose. "If true, we need to get to the bottom of it as soon as possible," he stressed. "We can't have a killer running amok on the parkway or anywhere in the Pisgah Ranger District."

"I understand," she told him. "We're utilizing all the resources at our disposal to come up with answers."

"Keep me posted."

"I will."

After disconnecting, Madison got out of her vehicle when she saw Law Enforcement Ranger Richard Edison drive up. He had been working on the parkway since transferring from the Commonwealth of Virginia, where he'd been a ranger at Shenandoah National Park, four months ago. Single and her age, he was flirtatious and wasn't bad looking but still not her type. He exited his car and approached her, tall and well built in his uniform. Beneath his campaign hat was a bleached-blond Caesar haircut. Sunglasses covered his blue eyes.

"Hey," he said in a level tone.

"Hey." She forced a smile.

"You okay?"

"No, not really," she confessed. "Our colleague was just murdered."

"Yeah, it sucks." His voice dropped an octave. "Nicole was a great ranger."

Madison smiled at the thought. "Yes, she was."

He paused. "You wanted to see me?"

She nodded, eyeing him. "Weren't you with Nicole earlier?"

"Yeah," he said readily. "We rode together for a bit, and then I let her out for foot patrol."

"Did you see anyone else hanging around at the time?"

"Yeah, lots of visitors and workers." Richard adjusted his glasses. "If you're asking if I saw anything unusual going on, the answer is no."

"Did Nicole indicate she was planning to meet with someone?" Madison asked.

"Not that I can recall." He leaned on one long leg. "I think she may have been dating someone, but I'm not sure."

Madison regarded him. "Did you ever go out with her?"

Richard's mouth creased. "No way. We were friends, but she was too young for me to date."

I'll have to take your word on that for now, Madison thought. "If you think of anything that might help in the investigation, let me know."

"I will." He jutted his chin. "I want whoever did this to Nicole to be brought to justice just as much as you do."

"Okay." Madison had no reason to believe this wasn't true. "See you later."

Next, she met up with Leonard at Julian Price Memorial Park, neighboring Moses H. Cone Memorial Park, at Milepost 297. He had been out questioning parkway visitors, with nearby road closures during the investigation given there was a killer at large.

"Hey," she said. "Get anything?"

"Nothing suspicious as yet," he reported. "Other than some sightings of the black bear, most people I spoke to apparently didn't hear or see anything that got their attention."

"Hmm…" Madison figured that Nicole would have screamed or made other sounds while being attacked. Could the perp have knocked her out first to prevent this? "Did Nicole ever say anything to you about being stalked by someone?"

"No." Leonard tilted his campaign hat. "We were cool but never talked about issues outside of working for the NPS and in the Blue Ridge Mountains."

"All right." She wondered if Nicole had known her attacker. Or if he'd known her. "Maybe someone will come forward with information."

"I'll let you know," he said.

As she headed back to her vehicle, Madison received a call from Ray Pottenger. "We've located the couple who first reported spotting the black bear," he informed her.

"That's great news," she told him.

"I'm sending you and Special Agent Sneed the address where you can find them."

"Okay." Madison reached her vehicle. Inside, she texted Garrett to let him know she was ready to follow up with the couple if he wanted her to interview them. Whatever it took to get the jump on Nicole's and, apparently, Olivia's killer.

Chapter Seven

Garrett drove to Linville Falls, in the Blue Ridge Mountains, at Milepost 316, where he located Maintenance Rangers Ward Wilcox and Ronnie Mantegna. They were picking up trash in the picnic area. Garrett hoped one or the other might have some useful information regarding the fatal attack on the parkway.

After bringing the men together, Garrett flashed his ID and said, "I'm investigating the murder of Park Ranger Nicole Wallenberg." He peered at Ronnie, who was in his midfifties, solid in build and had brownish-gray hair in a buzz cut and raven eyes. "When did you last see Ranger Wallenberg?"

"I saw her this morning," he responded. "She was with Ranger Edison, alive and well. Never saw either of them afterward."

Garrett took note of this. He turned to the other maintenance ranger. "What about you?"

Ward wiped sweat from his brow with the back of a work glove. "I saw Ranger Wallenberg on foot near where the black bear was located. She was alone. By the time Ranger Lynley arrived on the scene, Ranger

Wallenberg had moved farther into the woods, away from the area." He paused. "That must have been when she was attacked."

Garrett recalled that he had run into Drew Mitchell on the parkway, who'd been in possession of Olivia Forlani's cell phone, before fleeing. "Did you see anyone else in the vicinity of Ranger Wallenberg?"

"Yeah, as a matter of fact," Ward answered surely. "The couple who reported being confronted by the black bear had been hanging around that area earlier."

Garrett nodded and then handed both men his card. "If either of you see or hear about anything else pertinent to this investigation, give me a call."

"We will," Ronnie said, stuffing the card into the pocket of his shirt.

"Yeah, count on it," Ward seconded.

Garrett was already back in his car when he listened to the voice mail from Ray Pottenger, informing him that they had found the persons of interest in the death of Nicole. He texted their address. Garrett saw the text as well from Madison. He called her and, when she answered, said, "Hey. Got the text. We should check out the couple together and see where it leads."

"Sounds good to me," she told him. "Where are you?"

Garrett told her, and they arranged a place to meet. He welcomed any opportunity to spend time with Madison, on and off the job. And if it could help them crack what was becoming a more and more unsettling case, all the better.

THEY DROVE TO the Rolling Hills Bed and Breakfast on Danner Road, where Madison immediately recognized Stan and Constance Franco. They were standing outside the two-story Victorian. According to Deputy Pottenger, they were visiting from Honolulu. It was hard for Madison to imagine that they had decided in the middle of a vacation to the mainland to become killers along the way. But stranger things had happened.

"That's them," she told Garrett.

"Okay," he said. "Let's do this."

They exited the car and approached the couple. Both were in their late twenties, fit and good looking. Stan was tall, tanned, with slicked-back long hair in a man bun and brown eyes. Constance was nearly as tall and had big green eyes and fine blond hair in a short blunt cut, parted in the middle.

"Hi again," Madison said, after having spoken with them following the bear attack.

Constance smiled at her. "Hi."

"Ranger Lynley, right?" Stan said, eyeing her questioningly.

"Yes, and this is Special Agent Sneed," she told them. "We need to ask you a few questions."

"About the black bear?"

"Actually it's about a murder that took place on the Blue Ridge Parkway," Garrett said.

"Murder?" Constance grimaced. "Who?"

"A park ranger named Nicole Wallenberg," Madison informed them.

Garrett narrowed his eyes. "Someone stabbed

Ranger Wallenberg to death during the time you were on the parkway."

Stan pursed his lips. "I'm sorry to hear that," he said. "But you don't think we had anything to do with it, do you?"

"We're questioning everyone who was there or may have seen something," Madison answered evenly. She didn't want to frighten them unnecessarily. But there was never an easy way to confront potential suspects in crimes. "Ranger Wallenberg was killed not too far from the grassy area where you said you had a picnic. Did you hear or see anything?"

Constance's eyes darted to her husband's and back before responding, "Actually, around the time we spotted the black bear, there was what sounded like a woman crying out. But then the bear began making noises, and we thought that was what we heard."

Garrett regarded Stan keenly. "That true?"

"Yeah, it is," he insisted and turned to Madison. "When you showed up, along with the other rangers, to scare the bear off and nothing seemed to come of the other sounds, we assumed it was either our imagination or too much wine. Or the bear."

To Madison this seemed somewhat plausible, if convenient. "Did you see anyone leaving the area?" she asked, eyeing Constance.

"Yes." Her voice rose. "I saw a man running off in the woods."

"What did he look like?" Garrett asked.

She batted her lashes nervously. "I only noticed him at a glance, so I can't really tell you much about him. Honestly, I never gave it much thought one way or the other at the time. Sorry."

Madison turned to Stan. "Did you get a look at him?"

"Just the back of him as he was running into the forest," he told her. "I couldn't tell you anything else about him because he was too far away. And, to be honest, I don't know if he was trying to escape or just out for a jog."

"Neither do we," Garrett told him candidly. "But he's certainly someone we'd like to talk to."

"Afraid we can't help you there," he said.

Garrett looked at him. "How long will you be in town?"

"Till the end of the week."

"And you've been here for how long?"

"We arrived yesterday afternoon," Constance responded.

Stan frowned. "Why do you ask?"

"No reason in particular," Garrett answered, though Madison knew it was to establish an alibi for their whereabouts when Olivia had been killed. If this was true, it would eliminate them as suspects, making it less likely they could have been involved with Nicole's death. "In case we have any more questions, we'd like to get your contact information."

"Sure, no problem," he agreed.

Madison gazed at Constance and said smilingly, "Hope the ordeal with the black bear hasn't scared you off."

"Honestly, I'm still a bit shaken from it," she said.

"But it's even scarier to think that a murderer is apparently on the loose."

"Yeah," her husband grumbled. "Not exactly what we bargained for when deciding to vacation in North Carolina."

"None of us bargained for this—trust me," Garrett told him with an edge to his tone. "Unfortunately, things happen. Our job is to try to solve the case."

"Thanks for your time." Madison grinned at Stan. "We'll get out of your hair."

He nodded, and Constance said, "Thanks for coming to our rescue when the black bear didn't seem to want to leave us alone."

"Just doing my job," she said, diffident in accepting gratitude in this instance.

When they left, Garrett said, "What do you think?"

"I think they're innocent." Madison adjusted in the passenger seat. "Their alibi is easy enough to check out, if needed."

"True." He drove off. "If this man they saw running off is the real deal, then there's a good chance he was running away rather than toward something."

"Exactly." She faced him. "So, we really are looking at a likely serial killer?"

Garrett paused. "We'll see what the autopsy reveals on the cause and method of death," he voiced. "And what Forensics comes up with. But as of now, it seems like a distinct possibility."

"At least we have a solid lead to work with in trying to track down the perp," she pointed out.

"Yep. We just need a better description of the unsub in narrowing down the search."

Madison concurred. "Whoever he is, the unsub apparently knows his way around the Blue Ridge Parkway, if not the entire Pisgah National Forest," she speculated, what with his ability to avoid detection.

"I had that thought too." Garrett clutched the steering wheel. "Which makes him all the more dangerous."

Madison angled her face. "Are you thinking the unsub could be someone who works for the National Park Service?"

"Not necessarily. Apart from the many people employed by the NPS, there are plenty of regular visitors who are outdoorsmen, adventurers, hunters, survivalists, you name it, who choose to interact with nature in their life and times. Any one of them could have decided to become a killer along the way."

"Chilling," she uttered.

"Yeah." He drew a breath. "But we'll do whatever we have to in order to stop this from escalating," he told her.

Madison thought about her siblings investigating serial killers. She wondered how they managed to cope with the multiple lives lost at the hands of one or more killers. If they were suddenly dealing with this in her neck of the woods, she only hoped the unsub could be stopped in his tracks sooner rather than later. Having Garrett as lead investigator made her believe that this was a battle they would definitely win, no matter the obstacles before them.

When he pulled up behind her car, Garrett waited a beat, then turned toward Madison and leaned into her for a short kiss on the mouth. She felt her lips tingle, welcoming the kiss, but was still confused. "What was that for?"

"I just felt like kissing you," he responded point-blank. "Your lips are still as soft as I remember."

"Oh." She blushed but tried not to show it.

"Did I overstep?"

"No," she told him, realizing it was something that almost seemed inevitable, in spite of their attempts to place limitations on the nature of their relationship. But now was not the time to test those limits further. "I'll catch you later."

Garrett lowered his chin. "All right."

Madison exited his vehicle, sensing him watching until she had gotten into hers. He followed her briefly, till veering off in a different direction.

THOUGH IT HAD been quick and sweet, Garrett still had heart palpitations from kissing Madison when he walked inside his rented log cabin. He probably shouldn't have kissed her, aware that it could only lead them down a path they had mutually rejected before. But he didn't regret it. On the contrary, kissing her was maybe the best move he'd made since returning to Kiki's Ridge. He believed that Madison was amenable to it as well and that it was a step in the right direction toward reestablishing what had

existed between them before. Even if he had no idea
where they might be headed, one thing was clear to
him: he didn't want to let fear of failure be his guide.
What was meant to be would happen, one way or the
other. He preferred to control his own destiny, while
hoping it could align with hers.

After grabbing a beer from the refrigerator, Garrett broke away from thoughts about his personal
life in favor of the criminal investigation that had
shifted in a different direction somewhat with the
discovery of a second murder victim, Nicole Wallenberg. She had been isolated just long enough for
a killer to come after her. This was a similar pattern
to the stabbing murder of Olivia Forlani. Why had
the unsub targeted them? Or could they be separate
incidences with two different killers?

Either way he looked at it, Garrett knew that public confidence was bound to be eroded in the comfort level and security surrounding the Blue Ridge
Parkway for as long as safety was an issue. It was
up to him as the main investigator in this region to
solve these unsettling homicides. Or save the day.
While hardly a superhero, this was his forte as an
ISB special agent, and he didn't intend to let down
those who depended on him. That included Madison,
who had known one victim and discovered another
in the course of her own duties as a law enforcement
ranger. She needed to feel safe in her own workspace
without having to constantly look over her shoulder
for fear that a killer might be lying in wait.

IN THE MORNING, Garrett stuck with his routine of a jog and a workout to get the blood flowing. He hoped to get to do this with Madison soon, knowing that he had asked her to refrain from going out alone on the parkway trails as long as one or more killers were at large. He couldn't help but think about the ultimate workout they could have together in bed. Madison was a great lover, and it was one of the things he missed most about being with her. Would they get to experience the pleasure of one another's intimate company again? Or had that opportunity passed, in spite of a new understanding between them?

By the time he had gotten back to the cabin, showered and changed clothes, Dawn Dominguez had sent Garrett the autopsy report on Nicole Wallenberg. He read it on his laptop. The medical examiner confirmed that Nicole had been the victim of a vicious stabbing attack. She'd been stabbed ten times, including in the chest, stomach, back and arms, resulting in death as a homicide. He took note that, similar to Olivia's death, the undiscovered murder weapon was an eight-inch, single-edged blade knife characteristic of a survival knife.

I have to assume these homicides were perpetrated by the same offender, Garrett told himself while he drank his coffee. They were indeed facing a serial killer on the parkway. And the unsub had no qualms about stabbing his victims in a brazen daytime attack. This evoked thoughts once again to Garrett about his mother's murder in the same Blue Ridge Mountains thirty years ago. Who had gone after her and gotten away with it? He didn't want to think about history repeating itself with a new killer in the forest and mountains. Handpicking or having stalked his victims and never having to answer for it.

On his laptop, Garrett contacted his boss, Carly Tafoya, for a video chat to update her about the investigation. When she came on, he got right to the point. "There's been new developments to the case."

"Tell me," Carly voiced anxiously.

Having phoned her yesterday about the sad news of Nicole's murder and the speculation of its link to the murder of Olivia Forlani, Garrett said firmly, "We do think we have a serial killer on our hands. The autopsy report indicated that Nicole was stabbed to death in a way that mirrors Forlani's death, by and large. The murder weapon in both homicides is believed to be a survival knife."

Carly muttered an expletive while making a face. "That's not good."

"Not at all." Garrett frowned. "There's more. Witnesses reported seeing a man who may have been running from the scene of Nicole's murder. Though we haven't nailed down a solid description as yet, it fits with the strong suspicions on my part that the killer of Nicole and Olivia is male."

Carly sighed. "Use everything you have at your disposal, Sneed, to stop this man."

"I intend to," Garrett assured her.

"Whatever support you need, just ask."

"I will." As of now, what he needed most was to alert local and other federal law enforcement and communities in and around the Blue Ridge Parkway to be on guard for a likely serial killer on the loose. If they were able to at least rattle the cage somewhat of the unsub, it might be enough to force him to go underground and away from potential targets. Till they could nail him. And Garrett wouldn't rest till the deed was done.

Chapter Eight

Madison sat on the U-shaped bench in the breakfast nook, looking at the autopsy report that Garrett had sent her on her laptop. It was painful to read about the nature of and verdict on Nicole Wallenberg's death. Like Olivia, she'd been murdered by stabbing. A survival knife was thought to be the weapon of choice by the unsub. By all accounts, it seemed that they were looking at a serial killer and one who was elusive and violent enough to send a chill through Madison.

We can't let this monster get away with this, she told herself. Even then, the fear was that the longer it took to find the perp, the more likely it was that he would strike again.

She closed out the report and went onto Zoom for a video conference with her brothers, Scott and Russell Lynley. Both worked for the FBI as special agents, albeit in different capacities and locations. Scott was older and separated from his wife, Paula. Madison hoped they would be able to patch things up. Russell, who was younger, was married and about to bring a new Lynley into the world.

When they appeared on the screen, Madison broke into a grin, feeling comfort in talking with her brothers. Both were incredibly handsome and gray-eyed, much like their father. Scott had a square face and thick coal-black hair in a comb-over, low-fade style, while Russell had more of an oblong face to go with black hair in a high and tight cut.

"Hey, you two."

"Hey," they spoke in unison and paused before Scott said solemnly, "Heard you lost an NPS ranger."

"Yes, we did." Madison was not surprised that the news would reach them before she could pass it along. "Nicole was stabbed to death off the Blue Ridge Parkway," she said painfully.

"Sorry about that," Russell voiced, his thick brows knitted.

She twisted her lips. "Worse is that it comes on the heels of a similar death on the parkway of a friend of mine."

"Yeah, Annette mentioned that to me the other day. I reached out to you."

Madison acknowledged this and said, "It's certainly unsettling."

"So, what, we're talking about a serial killer lurking around in the Blue Ridge Mountains?" Scott put forth.

"Seems that way," she responded. "Between the location, manner of attack, type of injuries and the kind of knife believed to have been used to murder them, yes, I'd say a serial killer is at large."

Russell scratched his nose. "Who's heading the investigation?"

"Garrett Sneed," Madison answered equably.

Scott frowned. "Not the same ISB special agent who bailed on you?"

"One and the same," she admitted, though knowing it wasn't quite as simple as that.

"I thought he went to Arizona," Russell said. "Or was it New Mexico?"

"Did Sneed come back to give you more headaches?" Scott asked.

"Enough, already." Madison realized that they were just doing what overprotective brothers did in trying to look out for her best interests in their own ways. "Garrett and I are good." *Or at least no longer bad in terms of miscommunication*, she thought. "Anyway, this isn't about my love life. Or lack thereof. It's about Garrett coming in to do his job in investigating one, now two, homicides in the Pisgah Ranger District."

"You're absolutely right about that." Russell tilted his face. "He's obviously good at his job, as are you. Whatever you need to work out on a personal level, I'm sure you will."

She grinned. "Thanks for saying that."

He nodded. "We always have your back, sis."

In trying to lighten the mood, Scott said, "Still, if you ever need us to gang up on Sneed, we will."

Madison chuckled. "I don't think that will be necessary. He's one of the good guys."

"Okay." He sat back. "What can we do to help in the investigation?"

"Right now, I just need your support and an occasional virtual shoulder to cry on."

"You've got both," he said, and it was seconded by Russell.

Madison was grateful for such, knowing it worked both ways, as well as with Annette. When the chips were down, as Lynleys, they were there for each other, something she never took for granted.

After the chat ended, Madison got ready for work and headed for the parkway. Upon arrival, she parked and got out on foot and headed to the area where she'd found Nicole's body. The crime scene tape had been removed, allowing for free access. Though it was eerie to be back there, Madison thought she might check around for anything the crime scene techs and other rangers might have missed. It also occurred to her that the unsub might morbidly return to the scene of the crime. And even come after her.

Were the latter the case, she would be ready for him. Madison instinctively placed a hand on the firearm in her magnetic leather holster. In the meantime, if there was anything she could do to move the investigation along in trying to nab her fellow ranger's killer, she was up for the challenge.

Just as Madison was studying the dirt path Nicole would have taken to reach that point and happened to notice a fallen tree branch that she imagined could have been used to cover tracks, she heard what sounded like footsteps coming up fast behind her.

Sucking in a deep breath to suppress the fear that gripped her heart, Madison yanked out her pistol and flung herself around at the intruder, with no plans to ask questions first.

To her surprise, a hard question was posed to her instead, as the familiar deep voice barked, "What are you doing here?"

It took Madison only an instant to come to terms with the so-called intruder as actually Garrett. Releasing a sigh, she responded sardonically, "I work here, remember?"

"I remember." He put up his hands in mock surrender. "Don't shoot!"

Realizing she was still pointing the gun in his direction, she put it back in her holster. "Sorry about that. I thought you might be—"

"The killer?" Garrett deduced. "I gathered that much." He lowered his arms. "So you came to this spot in hopes of luring him out, or what?"

"No, I came in search of evidence," she told him matter-of-factly. "Seemed like a good place to start. After all, as you've reminded me more than once, this is my investigation too." Was she acting a bit too defensive? Was that really necessary?

"It is our investigation," he reiterated. "In fact, I made my way over here for the same reason. I was just surprised to find you here ahead of me."

Madison relaxed, feeling that she'd overreacted. "Guess great minds think alike," she quipped.

He grinned. "Did you find anything interesting?"

She took a few steps toward the tree branch, pulled

a latex glove out of her pocket and put it on, then picked up the branch. Turning it over, she saw a faint discoloration on one part. She held it up to him. "That could be human blood."

Garrett studied it. "Possibly."

"If so, it could belong to Nicole or the unsub," Madison said. "Forensics can tell us. If it is the killer's DNA, then CODIS might be able to identify the unknown DNA profile."

"You're right." He ran a hand along his jawline. "We'll get this to the state crime lab in Hendersonville," he said and looked at Madison curiously. "Did you find anything else?"

"Only that the area, largely hidden from the grassy hill and parking lot, suggests that the unsub made a conscious choice to either lure Nicole here or was lying in wait for anyone who happened to come to this spot to go after." Madison looked in a direction where the cluster of trees made for the perfect getaway. "He had to have gone that way to avoid detection for as long as possible."

"I think you're right." Garrett gave her the once-over, and she found herself coloring as she imagined he was undressing her with his very eyes—something she had admittedly found herself prone to doing with him from time to time since he'd returned. "We're checking dumpsters, trails, mountains and the water for the murder weapon and any bloody clothes the unsub may have ditched."

"Good." Madison hoped something would come up that pointed toward the perpetrator. She thought about Scott and Russell ribbing her about Garrett. In spite of their relationship being thrown off course for two years, Madison felt they were back on track now, even if it was unclear what train they were taking. Or, for that matter, what their next stop was.

When his cell phone rang, Garrett removed it from the back pocket of his chinos, looked at it and said, "I'd better get this." He answered, "Sneed," before saying, "Sheriff Silva. Yes, it has been a while. What can I do for you?"

Madison knew that Jacob Silva was the sheriff of Buncombe County, which bordered the Blue Ridge Parkway. She listened as Garrett lifted a brow and continued with, "Really?" Then, after a long pause, "Okay. Right. Good. Keep me posted."

When Garrett disconnected, he eyed her and said, "There's been a development…"

"What?" Her voice rose with interest.

His mouth tightened. "A woman was stabbed to death this morning in Buncombe County. The suspect, identified as Norman Kruger, carjacked another woman's vehicle and is currently on the move in her blue Hyundai Elantra." Garrett waited a beat and said tonelessly, "Silva thinks that Kruger could be the unsub, who the local press is now referring to as the Blue Ridge Parkway Killer."

GARRETT STOOD TOE-TO-TOE with Sheriff Jacob Silva, whom he'd known since his previous stint as a Region 2 ISB special agent. They were the same height, but Silva was a little heavier. In his midforties, he had brown eyes and short brown hair with a sprinkling of gray and a horseshoe mustache.

"What can you tell me about the suspect?" Garrett asked as they stood outside an interrogation room at the sheriff's office in Asheville, where thirty-four-year-old Norman Kruger was waiting to be interviewed. An hour ago, he had been taken into custody without incident after a high-speed chase had come to an end when he'd lost control of the car. Though shaken up, the carjacking victim, seventy-three-year-old Diane Fullerton, had been unharmed.

"Kruger is a real piece of work," Silva told him. "He's been in and out of jail for most of his life for crimes ranging from larceny-theft to aggravated assault to kidnapping and drug possession. He's currently being charged with first-degree murder in the death of thirty-two-year-old Frances Reynolds, thought to be the girlfriend of the suspect. She was stabbed multiple times and left for dead in her apartment. He's also facing charges of armed carjacking, unlawful use of a weapon and resisting arrest. Other charges are pending. And, obviously, there could be more, after your interrogation of the suspect."

"What about the murder weapon?"

"We collected as evidence a survival knife that we believe was the weapon he used to stab to death Frances Reynolds. It's being processed right now."

"Good," Garrett said, thoughtful. "I'll take it from here."

Silva nodded. "He's all yours."

When he stepped inside the room, Garrett knew

that Madison would be watching the interrogation on live video in a different room with interest, hoping, like him, that they had the man responsible for the cold-blooded murders of Olivia Forlani and Nicole Wallenberg. He turned his attention back to the suspect, who was seated at a square metal table and handcuffed, and told him, "I'm Special Agent Sneed of the National Park Service's Investigative Services Branch."

Norman Kruger was lean, wearing a dirty T-shirt and jeans. He had dark hair in a skin-fade cut with the top textured. Snarling at Garrett, he retorted, "So what do you want with me?"

Garrett sat in a metal chair across from him and glared at the suspect. "Why don't we start by discussing why you're here," he began coolly. "You're facing a murder rap in the stabbing death of Frances Reynolds, among other charges."

"Tell me something I don't know." He jutted his chin. "That bitch had it coming to her after two-timing on me with another dude."

"What about the elderly woman who nearly had a heart attack when you ordered her out of her vehicle at gunpoint?" Garrett peered at him. "Did she have it coming too?"

"I needed some wheels," Kruger hissed. "She was just in the way."

I'll bet, he mused cynically. "Didn't get you very far for where you're going from here. Did it?"

Kruger twisted his lips. "Whatever."

He sighed, knowing it was time to confront the

smug suspect over the homicides that had occurred on the parkway. "Why don't we talk about the two women murdered recently on the Blue Ridge Parkway," he said casually, noting the suspect had not asked for an attorney.

Kruger stared at him with a furrowed brow. "Not sure what you mean?"

"I'll try to clarify," Garrett snapped. "You're being investigated as a person of interest in the murders of Olivia Forlani and Nicole Wallenberg. Both were stabbed to death in separate incidents along trails off the parkway, reminiscent of your attack on Frances Reynolds."

"Hey, I had nothing to do with those."

Garrett bristled with skepticism. "Someone fitting your description was seen running off after murdering Park Ranger Nicole Wallenberg yesterday morning," he pointed out. In reality, Garrett knew that the description of the unsub was pretty vague at best. But Kruger didn't need to know that at the moment. Especially if this helped lead to a confession when he was backed into a proverbial corner.

"Wasn't me," Kruger maintained. He wrinkled his crooked nose. "I wasn't anywhere near the parkway yesterday."

Garrett dismissed this with a wave of his hand. "So where were you?"

"I was in Charlotte," he argued.

"Doing what?"

"Playing at a dive bar called the Parties Pad," Kruger said. "I play guitar with a band that travels around the state and elsewhere. Did three sets and played pool afterward. I have witnesses. Didn't get back here till early this morning, after hitching a ride with another member of the band—Chuck Garcia. So no, you can't pin the ranger's death on me."

Garrett looked at the camera, wondering what Madison's take was on the suspect. Was this another dead end? He regarded Kruger. "We'll check out your story." He paused and then asked for his whereabouts during the time of Olivia Forlani's murder, not ruling out that there might still have been more than one killer at work.

Kruger again claimed he'd been on the road with his band, giving dates and places they'd performed. It would be easy enough to verify. Garrett still had his suspicions, though, and asked Kruger if he would be willing to take a lie detector test. "It'll help us rule you out for the parkway murders," he told the suspect.

"Yeah, whatever." Kruger shrugged. "But you're wasting your time. As I said, I never killed anyone on the Blue Ridge Parkway."

Garrett leaned forward. "That remains to be seen."

He left the interrogation room and arranged with Sheriff Silva to have the test administered by a polygraph examiner before going to confer with Madison in a viewing room.

"So, what do you think about Kruger?" he asked her.

"He's definitely a creep," she stated flatly. "But I'm not sure he's guilty of being the Blue Ridge Parkway Killer. He seemed too arrogant and clear in his denials."

Garrett was inclined to agree. "We'll see if he passes the lie detector test and if the knife he used to kill his girlfriend yields anything."

Madison folded her arms. "If nothing else, at least they got him for what he did to her."

"Yeah."

Sheriff Silva entered the room and said with a frown on his face, "The polygraph examiner is on her way. In the meantime, we can add attempted murder to the growing list of charges Kruger faces. Just received word that he practically beat to death a man named Peter McLachlan. Kruger's girlfriend was apparently having an affair with McLachlan. Looks like he'll pull through, but he's got a long haul ahead of him."

Madison grimaced. "Kruger was clearly a loose cannon with others paying the price."

Garrett shook his head in despair. "He definitely went off the deep end in his homicidal vengeance."

"And he's going to pay for it," Silva said with certainty. "The only question left is whether or not we can pin the parkway crimes on him."

"There is that," Garrett conceded, but he only wanted things to go in that direction if Kruger was actually guilty of the serial murders.

Two hours later, they were informed that Norman Kruger had passed the polygraph and that his alibis checked out. Forensic testing of the survival knife used to kill Frances Reynolds had found no DNA or blood evidence to tie the weapon to Olivia or Nicole. Moreover, the blade of Kruger's knife measured just four inches, compared to the eight-inch knife the killer had used against Forlani and Wallenberg. This was more than enough for Garrett to move away from Norman Kruger as a suspect, even as the book was thrown at him for the murder of his girlfriend and other offenses.

Chapter Nine

"What do you say we split a pizza?" Garrett offered that evening as he rode with Madison.

"Sure," she responded, her stomach growling after missing lunch. "Takeout?"

"Yeah. Unless you'd rather eat at the restaurant?"

"Takeout is fine."

"All right. Takeout it is."

Madison took the Blue Ridge Parkway to Beaubianna Drive, where she pulled into the Dottie's Pizza parking lot.

"So, what would you like on your half?" Garrett asked, unbuckling his seat belt.

Had he forgotten that she loved pepperoni, anchovies and cheese pizza? She grinned at him. "Surprise me."

"I can do that." He returned the smile. "Back in a few."

While she waited, Madison wondered if there could still be a future for them. Or had that ship sailed and there was no need to think in terms beyond camaraderie and working together on a case?

She was still mulling this over when Garrett returned. "All set?"

"Yeah. I think you'll be pleased with the selection of toppings for your half."

"Can't wait to taste it." The inviting aroma of the pizza made her stomach growl again.

"So, your place or mine?" he asked casually.

"Hmm…" Madison contemplated this. "Mine. There's beer and wine in the fridge to help wash down the pizza." Never mind that the place was her own comfort zone.

Garrett grinned. "Sounds fine to me."

They were mostly silent during the drive, except the occasional comment on the landscape or something new that Garrett noted along the way from when he'd lived in the area previously.

When they reached her house and went inside, he hit the lights, scanned the place and said, "Looks pretty much like I remember."

Madison batted her eyes. "Did you think it would have changed?"

"Not really. Sometimes people do like to redecorate or whatever, just for the hell of it. In this case, the house is perfect just as it is."

"Thanks." *He always had a way with words*, she thought, smiling. Madison took the pizza box from him and said, "I'll set everything out. Make yourself at home."

"I'd like to help," he insisted, following her into the kitchen.

"Okay," she relented, handing him back the pizza.

"We can eat at the dining room table. Napkins are in that drawer—" she pointed "—in case you've forgotten."

"I remember." After washing and drying his hands, he grabbed a batch of napkins and headed into the dining room.

Madison washed up. "Did you want beer or red wine?" she asked, taking a couple of plates out of the rustic cabinet.

"Beer."

She'd suspected as much. After setting the plates on the mahogany square table, she got out two bottles from the refrigerator. Handing him one, she sat across from him in an upholstered gray side chair. Madison noted that the pizza box was still closed.

She gazed at Garrett, who was grinning sideways as he said to her, "I'll let you do the honors."

When she lifted the lid, Madison broke into a smile as she saw that the entire pizza was covered with pepperoni, anchovies and cheese. He'd remembered. "Cute," she uttered, blushing.

He laughed. "Hey, some memories never go away."

And others? She wondered just how much he recalled about their previous time spent as a couple. "Good to know."

They began to eat and drink while talking about the investigation. "Too bad Norman Kruger didn't pan out as our killer," Garrett bemoaned.

"I know." Madison dug into a slice of pizza. His disappointment matched her own. "At least Kruger is off the streets for his own horrific crimes."

"Yeah, you're right about that." Garrett sipped his beer. "As for the Blue Ridge Parkway Killer, as they're calling him, with the technology we have working for us, he's not about to slip through the cracks."

"Something tells me he doesn't want to," she surmised. "At least not totally. If the unsub was willing to kill two women on the parkway, there's no telling how many more he's capable of killing, if the opportunity is there. Clearly, he's able and willing."

"And we're just as able to come between him and his dastardly plans," Garrett insisted. "We're onto him now, and he knows it. Homing in on other vulnerable women just got much more difficult for him, if he hopes to remain in the shadows instead of behind bars."

"I want that to be true." She took another bite of pizza. "This can't go on for much longer. Not if we want to restore sanity to the Blue Ridge Parkway. And the rest of the Pisgah National Forest, for that matter."

"It won't." Garrett's voice deepened with conviction. He suddenly reached across the table and ran a finger down the corner of her mouth. "Some cheese had managed to get away from you. Thought I'd help out there."

Her face flushed with embarrassment. Or was it more of a turn-on to feel the touch of his finger? "A napkin would have sufficed, thank you."

He cut a grin. "Maybe. But what fun would that have been?"

"I thought we were here to eat. Not have fun."

"Why not do both?" Garrett bit into his own pizza slice and seemed to deliberately allow a web of cheese to hang down his chin. "Think I could use a little help here," he said, a catch to his voice.

"Oh, really?" Madison played along and used her own finger to wind around the cheese before removing it. "Satisfied?"

He stood up and took her hand, pulling her up. "Actually, I'm not quite satisfied, not yet."

They were close enough that she could feel the heat emanating from him. "And what else did you have in mind?"

"This…" Garrett held Madison's cheeks and planted his mouth on her lips for a solid kiss. It felt good and neither seemed in any hurry to stop kissing one another.

When she finally unlocked their mouths, Madison looked him in the eye and saw the desire, which she felt too. "Are you sure this is a good idea?" she asked, wondering if he would be the voice of reason before things went too far to pull back.

"I'm sure it's an idea that's long overdue," he indicated. "Yes, I want to kiss you some more and then make love to you, Madison."

"I think I want that too," she admitted, quivering at the thought. "Yes, I do want it," Madison felt the need to make clear.

"So, let's do this." He regarded her keenly and took her hand. "I think I remember how to get to the bedroom."

"I'm sure you do." She smiled as her heart skipped a beat. "Lead the way."

Once they stepped inside the room, Garrett stopped and said, "There's something else I've been dying to do since I laid eyes on you again…"

She held his gaze with anticipation. "Oh? What's that?"

"This," he said as he unraveled her hair from the bun it was in, allowing it to fall freely upon her shoulders. He tousled the hair. "I love your long locks."

Madison knew this, but they had not been in the right situation for her to wear it down. Till now. "Kiss me," she demanded, grabbing his shirt.

"With pleasure."

They stood there, kissing one another like old lovers, which Madison knew they were. This both frightened and excited her. More the latter, as the intensity of the kiss grew as their bodies molded together while they wrapped their arms around each other. She was all in for the ride, even if the future remained uncertain.

After they shed their clothes with lightning speed, removing any barriers between them, Madison felt just a tad self-conscious in baring all to a man for the first time since their relationship had ended.

But this quickly went away with the sheer appreciation she saw in his stare that he followed with, "You're still gorgeous."

Drinking in the sight of his hard body and six-pack, causing a stir in her, she couldn't help but say in response, "So are you, Garrett."

"I'll take that, coming from you." He stepped closer and lifted up her chin. "And give this in return." Another mouth-watering kiss was laid on her, making Madison feel as though she were floating on air. When it came time for them to take this to bed, she removed a condom packet from the nightstand that had not yet expired.

Handing it to him, she smiled and said, "From the last time you were here."

Garrett chuckled. "Glad you saved it."

"So am I." Madison gazed at him desirously. "Better not let it go to waste."

"Oh, it won't," he promised, tossing the packet onto the bed to come back to later. "First things first."

Her lashes fluttered with anticipation. "What might that be?"

Garrett kissed her forehead. "A little of this…" He kissed both cheeks. "A little of that…" He ran his hands through her hair while kissing her on the mouth. "Maybe some of that and this…" He touched one nipple, then the other, causing waves of delight to shoot through Madison. It caused her desire to be with him to kick up another fervent notch.

"I get the picture," she cooed impatiently, taking his hand and leading him to the bed. "Let's move on…please."

"Got it." His voice rang with conviction as they got on the sateen duvet cover. He draped one leg across hers. "Before we get down to business, I'd like us to reacquaint ourselves with one another."

"Oh, would you now?" Madison kissed him, moving her hand down his body teasingly as he stiffened. "I'm sensing some familiarity here."

"So am I." Garrett had a sharp intake of breath as his nimble fingers went to work on her, finding all the right intimate spots. "And I'm liking what I'm feeling."

"Umm…me too," she voiced dulcetly, body suddenly ablaze as an orgasm roared through her. When she couldn't take the pure torture of a partial victory anymore, Madison demanded, "I'd like to feel even more of you inside me. Now!"

"As you wish," he said, kissing her mouth again before ripping open the packet and putting on the condom.

But even as she longed for further fulfillment, Garrett once again showed enormous patience for his own needs as he stimulated her more before finally moving atop and working his way between her legs. Ready as ever, Madison was definitely hot and bothered when he entered her. She absorbed his quick and powerful thrusts the way the skin did the sun's rays, meeting him halfway each time.

Their mouths were locked passionately as their bodies moved in perpetual harmony. In short order, Madison climaxed again, at the same time as Garrett. She could feel the erratic beating of his heart, matching her own as the moment came and left them catching their breaths afterward.

"Wow." Garrett laughed as he lay on his back beside her. "That—you—were amazing."

"So were you," Madison admitted, resting her head on his shoulder.

"Some things in life are worth waiting for—again."

She chuckled. "You think so?"

"I know so." He kissed her hair. "This was definitely worth a two-year wait. Every scintillating second."

Though she didn't disagree, Madison was left to wonder what came next. Did he even know? Should it be an issue?

"WHAT ARE WE DOING?" Madison asked him as she propped up on an elbow, giving Garrett a nice view of her nude body.

He pretended he didn't get her drift as he took in her perfectly sized breasts, shapely form and long lean legs, while quipping, "I should think it would be obvious. It's called jumping each other's bones."

She laughed and hit him playfully on the shoulder. "You know what I mean."

He did and, as such, turned serious when facing her, while considering how best to respond without overpromising or understating where they were. "Well, I think we're simply reconnecting in one way in which we were crazy for one another," he spoke honestly. "Seems like it worked out pretty well. Don't you think?"

"Hmm…" Madison met his eyes thoughtfully. "What happened to just being friends?"

Garrett held her gaze when he responded dubiously, "Friendship comes in many forms."

"And what form would you call this?" she asked. "Friendship with benefits?"

He laughed. "I think I'd be more comfortable with friendship and the enormous possibilities it presents for a brighter future between us, in one way or another."

Okay, I came out with where I'd like to see this go, sort of, Garrett told himself. He hoped they were on the same page.

Madison raised a brow. "That doesn't scare you?"

"It might have once," he confessed. "But not now. I'm open to whatever comes next. You?"

She waited a beat and then said evenly, "Yeah, I think I am."

"Cool." He beamed and, taking in her scent, suddenly felt himself aroused again. Running a hand across her back, he asked, "Are there any more of those packets in the nightstand?"

"There might be one or two more. Why?"

"Oh, I was thinking it might be fun to go a second round."

Her eyes lit. "Really?"

He grinned. "Well, things did go a bit more quickly than I would have liked," he admitted.

"I see." She touched his chest. "Sure you can handle another round?"

He chuckled. "Without a doubt. Being with you gives me all the energy I need."

"Then I say let's go for it," she said enthusiastically.

This was music to Garrett's ears as he started to

kiss her, slipping his tongue in Madison's mouth. He absolutely loved the taste and feel of her, making him want her even more. By the time they had worked each other up into a near frenzy, he had managed to slip out of bed just long enough to put on the protection before picking up where they'd left off. Their bodies were entangled in the heat of passion and exploration.

Madison moaned as he hit her sweet spot time and time again, then called out his name when she reached orgasm while on top. Having held back just long enough to wait for that to happen, Garrett played with her hair and brought their faces together for a toe-curling kiss before letting go in achieving his own pinnacle of sexual gratification. Only then did they settle down and ride the rapids of contentment.

"Was it just as good the second time?" Madison asked with a giggle. "Not counting our previous love-making sessions."

Garrett grinned slyly beside her. "What do you think?"

"Umm… I think so, judging by how wonderful it was for me."

"Good deduction." His voice deepened. "You never fail to amaze me just how incredible you are in bed."

Her eyes narrowed. "Just in bed?"

He chuckled, realizing how what he'd said might have come across. "In and out of bed," he promised. "Breaking up had nothing to do with how great you are as a person." He hoped she knew that.

"I could say the same about you," she told him while running her fingers over his chest.

"Yeah?"

"Of course. You've always been able to capture my fancy, Special Agent Sneed, even when we were no longer together."

"I'll take capturing your fancy anytime," he said lightheartedly but meant every word.

"Oh, really?" Madison brushed her lips against his. "If you think you can handle a third go at it, I'm game."

He laughed. "You're insatiable, you know that?"

"And you're not?"

"Guilty as charged." Garrett couldn't keep a big smile off his face. He loved being able to take his time in pleasuring Madison and being pleasured by her. It was the one sure area where they clicked on all levels. The fact that it felt so natural, as if not missing a beat, didn't surprise him. Hell, he'd never felt for one instant that their lovemaking wouldn't be everything it had been before. But he'd been wrong. The sex was better than ever between them. This told him that she'd been the one thing missing in his life for two years that had left him feeling a void. Now that they had rekindled things, he wasn't about to let what they had slip through his fingers again.

The fact that they were still dealing with an unsub serial killer on the parkway was troubling for sure. But Garrett was as equally committed to having a second shot with Madison as he was to stopping the murders on the Blue Ridge Parkway. Something he had never been able to do to save his mother from falling prey to a bad man.

Chapter Ten

"Are you up for a run this morning?" Madison asked, wanting to take advantage of Garrett's presence after halting her runs temporarily while a killer was on the loose. Of course, she knew he was in her bed, naked, and hadn't brought any jogging attire after spending the night. Whereas she had been up for half an hour, made coffee and, after putting her hair into a high ponytail, had thrown on a sports bra, running shorts and sneakers.

Rubbing his eyes of sleepiness, Garrett replied, "Yeah, sure. We can pop over to my cabin, and I'll get dressed for a run. There's a great trail there. Then we can have breakfast there, back here or wherever you like."

"Sounds good." Madison smiled at him, feeling a fresh surge of desire after getting little sleep. But she kept it in check, not wanting to read too much into what had happened between them—in spite of the indication by both of them that it was a building block for a renewed relationship, rather than an exciting trip down memory lane. The last thing she wanted was to end up disappointed once more. "I'll wait for you downstairs," she said, not trusting herself in getting too cozy again.

"Okay," he said simply, sitting up. "I won't be long."

Twenty minutes later, they were running along a trail meandering between bigtooth aspen, tulip and magnolia trees. Madison managed to keep pace with Garrett, who had changed into a blue T-shirt and running shorts—with his muscular arms and legs in full display—and training sneakers. She studied him. He seemed caught up in his own world, in spite of having regained a place in hers.

"You don't talk much about your mother," Madison tossed at him for some reason. In their previous relationship, she'd only been given a general accounting of what had happened to her and him thereafter. Madison wanted more but didn't feel it was her place to ask.

Garrett gazed at her thoughtfully and said, "Kind of a hard thing to talk about, you know?"

"Yeah, I get that." She acknowledged that it wasn't so easy to think about her own parents' tragic death, much less air out her feelings about losing them too soon in life. But given the way his mother had died and his own shattered childhood as a result, it was still different. "Might help, though, to share what it is you're feeling. I know it's been a long time having to carry the memory of her death."

"You're right." He took a breath. "I want to let you in on what I've been carrying around for thirty years." Another sigh. "With no father in the picture, my mother, as a single parent, meant the world to me. She taught me everything she could to a five-year-old about the Cherokee culture but not nearly what she would have, had she lived longer."

Madison flashed him a sympathetic look. "I can only imagine how much it took out of you to have been deprived of this."

"Though she's been gone a long time, I still find myself trying to come to terms with the lost opportunity," he stated musingly. "The fact that her killer was never found only makes it worse."

"Which I know is only exacerbated by the current case we're working on," she voiced sadly.

Garrett nodded, wiping his brow with the back of his hand. "Yeah. But I can't go back and undo what was done to my mother. Hard as it is, I have to live for today. That includes my job. And getting to spend time with you again."

Madison took solace in his words and was encouraged by them. "I feel the same way."

He gave her a thin smile and said, "Better head back now."

"Okay." She took the lead and stayed just ahead of him as they navigated the trail and were silent while listening to the sounds of nature all around them.

GARRETT FELT BETTER in sharing his thoughts about his mother with Madison and having been raised by his grandparents. As someone he wanted to play an important part in his life, he understood that this included being open about his history and their own potential future beyond a serial-murder investigation. In turn, he needed just as much from her if they were to have a chance in making this work.

That morning, they met up with Leonard along the parkway. His brow creased as he said, "A couple of the maintenance rangers found a blood-soaked shirt and a survival knife buried in a dumpster."

Madison reacted with interest. "Really?"

"Yeah. They were apparently in a black plastic bag and underneath other trash, as if by design."

"And where was the dumpster located?" Garrett asked curiously.

"Not far from the Blue Ridge National Heritage Area," Leonard answered.

"Hmm…" He pondered this. "If this proves to be what we think it is, that would mean the unsub went the extra mile, so to speak, to try to hide evidence of one or more murders."

"Yeah, looks that way to me," Leonard concurred.

"Where are these items now?" Madison asked the ranger.

"Turned them over to the crime lab for processing."

"Good," Garrett told him. "We need to know, like yesterday, if this is a solid lead or not."

Leonard nodded. "I hear you."

"Makes sense that the unsub in one or both murders would try to unload the evidence of the crimes," Madison said. "Especially as the investigation heats up."

"We'll see," Garrett said, preferring to reserve judgment for now, while remaining optimistic that this was a potential breakthrough development.

Two hours later, he and Madison drove to the Western Regional Crime Laboratory in Hendersonville on Saint Pauls Road. There, they met with Jewel Yasumori, a slender, thirtysomething forensic analyst, for the results on testing of the items recovered. Earlier, she had been sent the tree branch that Madison had found near the spot where Nicole had been murdered.

Garrett was impatient as he looked at Jewel, whose short black hair was in a pixie bob with tapered sideburns. He asked point-blank, "What did you learn from analyzing the shirt and survival knife?"

Jewel blinked dark brown eyes and said, "Let's start with the shirt." She turned on her monitor that had an image of a man's casual button-down blue shirt. It was stained with blood. "We tested the blood for DNA and found that it was a match for Ranger Nicole Wallenberg's DNA."

Garrett watched Madison's jaw drop with the confirmation before she asked, "Did you find anyone else's DNA on the shirt?"

"Afraid not," Jewel said. "However, we were able to gather some fibers from the shirt as trace evidence. They were consistent with fibers found on Ranger Wallenberg's clothing, which can further be used to make a case against the unsub."

Garrett took note of that and asked her with interest, "What about the knife?"

Jewel's brow creased as she pulled up an image of a survival knife on her display. It had a rubber handle. "We found blood stains on the stainless-steel survival knife with a single-edged blade that measured eight inches. They matched the DNA profiles of Nicole Wallenberg and Olivia Forlani," she told them. "As such, this was almost certainly the weapon used to kill both of them."

Madison wrinkled her nose in disgust. "The perp was so brazen as to keep the same knife to go after Olivia, then Nicole."

"But smart enough to get rid of it rather than take a chance that the weapon might be discovered on his person or property," Garrett surmised. What concerned him was the unsub getting another survival knife to carry on his killings. "Were you able to pull any prints off the knife?"

"Actually, we do have some positive news on that front." Jewel perked up. "We were able to recover a latent palm print from a right hand off the knife," she reported enthusiastically. "It was entered into the FBI's Next Generation Identification system biometric database with its Advanced Fingerprint Identification Technology and the State Bureau of Investigation's Computerized Criminal History file." She sighed. "Unfortunately, we haven't been able to get a hit as yet on the unsub, if he's in the system."

Garrett frowned. He had to consider that the perp might somehow have been able to avoid arrest or incarceration, keeping his prints from being on file. "So, no DNA potentially belonging to the unsub?" he had to ask.

"We're still probing for this." Jewel licked her lips.

"It's possible that we might be able to obtain a partial DNA profile of the unsub from the palm print or the part of the knife where it was left. This will depend on the number of cells we can gather from the latent print." She paused. "Of course, if we can retrieve an unknown DNA profile, we'll be able to upload it to CODIS and see if there's a match to an arrestee or offender or DNA profile."

"That's a lot of ifs," Madison pointed out skeptically. "But at least it gives us something to work with in going after the unsub."

"My sentiments exactly," Garrett said, believing that either way he looked at it, they were a step or two closer to identifying the Blue Ridge Parkway Killer. "For instance, we've now confirmed, more or less, that a single perpetrator was responsible for the stabbing deaths of Olivia Forlani and Nicole Wallenberg. And that he's running scared in trying to bury the evidence of his crimes."

Jewel nodded and said, "Forensics has a way of allowing us to catch up to unsubs, no matter their efforts to the contrary."

"Amen to that," Madison uttered, eyeing Garrett.

"Yeah, we're thankful for that," he concurred before they headed back to the parkway, having made progress in their endeavors of solving two homicides.

MADISON AGREED THAT forensic evidence linking the murders of Olivia and Nicole to one assailant was a breakthrough in the case. Whether this would be enough to identify the unsub remained to be seen.

But at least they seemed to be headed in the right direction, even if it was still frustrating that the serial killer remained at large for the time being.

We just need to find him before he goes after someone else, she told herself while riding back to the parkway with Garrett. Like her, he was caught up in his own thoughts. Madison imagined that these meandered back and forth between his own past family tragedy and determination to prevent the present-day killer from becoming tomorrow's cold case. As for their own evolving relationship, she was willing to take it one day at a time and see where it went, while trying her best not to presume their history would repeat itself and leave them both unsatisfied.

That cloudy afternoon, a memorial service was held for Nicole Wallenberg at Julian Price Memorial Park. Attendees included park rangers and other NPS employees and volunteers. All had come to pay their respects for whom Madison believed had been a dedicated worker who'd given her all to the job.

Garrett and her boss approached Madison as she stood alongside Leonard and other rangers. "How are you holding up?" Tom asked her in a sympathetic tone.

"Just trying to get through this," Madison confessed, something that had never become routine to her.

"You will," he said, his voice filled with confidence. "In the meantime, we'll do all we can to bring Nicole justice."

"To that effect," Garrett said, brushing against

Madison's shoulder, "my boss has approved offering a twenty-five-thousand-dollar reward for any info that leads to the arrest and conviction of Nicole's killer. Which obviously will give us justice as well for Olivia Forlani."

Madison's eyes lit. "That's good to know. Hopefully this will motivate someone to do the right thing, even if it takes a cash reward to make that happen."

"It's been a proven means of loosening lips," he told her.

"You never know how these things will go," Tom spoke realistically. "But between Carly and myself, we're committed to leaving no stone unturned in solving this case. Rewards are often a last resort, but we want to jump on the momentum we have going for us. That includes showing images of the shirt worn by the unsub in the hope that someone in the public will recognize it, along with a vague description of the man seen running into the woods."

Leonard added, "We're also interviewing people who may have seen someone hanging out by the dumpster around the time shortly after Nicole was murdered."

Madison nodded. "Looks like we have the bases covered in trying to nab the unsub. Now it only needs to happen."

"We just have to let the system play itself out," Garrett told her evenly.

"Right." She met his eyes, tempering her eagerness to give Nicole the peace in death that she deserved.

"I wouldn't be surprised if we're inundated with

leads shortly," he contended. "It only takes one to blow this thing wide open."

Madison concurred, and then turned her attention to some rangers who stood at a podium to say a few words on behalf of Nicole. One was Ward Wilcox, the maintenance ranger who'd been present when Madison had gotten the black bear to run off into the woods and leave parkway visitors alone. She was surprised at his heartfelt words about Nicole, whom he described as someone who could have been his daughter. These sentiments were echoed by maintenance worker Ronnie Mantegna, who said, "Nicole struck me as someone who only wanted to make a difference. For some bastard to take that away from her is reprehensible. Whoever did it needs to be held accountable."

I couldn't agree more, a voice in Madison's head told her. They all had a responsibility to come together on behalf of Nicole and Olivia in not letting the unsub get away with cold-blooded murder. It appeared as if they were doing just that. She gazed at Garrett, who seemed to be reading her mind and gave her a look of resolve in seeing this through.

After Leonard spoke to the gathering, it was Madison's turn to step to the podium. She took a moment or two to collect her thoughts before honoring Nicole's life and what she'd stood for as a park ranger. Though they hadn't exactly been friends as far as hanging out together, with Madison being older, but she'd been on friendly terms with Nicole and had occasionally offered her career advice, and they'd shared some anecdotes about ranger life. In Madison's book, that counted for something that she would carry with her for the rest of her life. Just as she would the brief time she'd gotten to know Olivia before her life had also been cut short by a ruthless killer.

Chapter Eleven

That evening, Madison did some house cleaning, feeling the need to keep her mind preoccupied. It was her proven strategy for dealing with the difficult parts of being a law enforcement ranger and not become overwhelmed by it. *I can take it, but I'm still human too*, she told herself. Something she always tried to keep in a proper perspective when having alone time.

As for Garrett, neither of them had rushed into a repeat performance from last night. Passionate and pleasurable as it was to make love, she didn't want to overdo it at the expense of having something real that went well beyond the bedroom. She sensed that Garrett felt the same way, respecting him for that. If they were to make it work this time, great sex would only be part of the equation, with a happy balance between personal and career lives essential to success.

When she got a call from Annette, Madison stopped dusting and took the video chat while standing in the kitchen.

"Hey," her sister greeted her.

"Hi." Madison smiled. "Thanks for rescuing me from my chores."

Annette laughed. "Actually, I could say the same about you. I needed an excuse to take a break."

She chuckled. "I'll gladly give you that."

"So, what's happening with you and Garrett? Or shouldn't I ask?"

"You may." Madison grinned. "Let's just say that we're working on getting back together."

"Hmm…" Annette's eyes widened. "Does that mean you're putting in plenty of overtime 'reacclimating yourselves to one another'?"

She colored. "We're taking one step at a time," she told her diplomatically.

"Okay." Her sister sat back. "What's the latest on your investigation?"

Madison brought her up to speed on where things stood, then finished with, "All hands are on deck, Annette, as we try to put the squeeze on the unsub."

"You'll get him," she spoke with confidence. "Having been there, done that last year, it's not something I'd wish on my worst law enforcement enemy. Much less my big sister. But between you and Garrett, along with the support staff, I have no doubt that an arrest of the culprit is imminent."

Madison flashed her teeth. "Since when did you become so much like Mom and Dad?" she teased her, still remembering when Annette had first become part of their family when brought home from the adoption agency, and had been instantly adored, proving that she belonged.

"Look who's talking." She laughed. "I think our parents left an indelible mark on all of us."

"I agree." They talked a little about Annette's married life and their brothers before they said their goodbyes.

Madison returned to cleaning the house and then took a nice relaxing bubble bath. There, she couldn't help but recall the times when she and Garrett had played footsie and explored one another in the tub during their previous relationship and then made their way to bed for some great sex. Suddenly feeling aroused, she quickly shut off those thoughts and considered what tomorrow would bring in their investigation of a deadly unsub.

THE FOLLOWING DAY, while looking over data on the case at his log cabin, Garrett got word about a disturbing text the ISB tip line had received in relation to the Blue Ridge Parkway killings. The National Park Service routinely received hundreds, if not thousands, of tips from the public annually on various crimes and otherwise suspicious activities that took place in national parks. Every one of these was taken seriously and, when appropriate, investigated. Normally, he would have passed this off to local park rangers. But upon being sent and reading the text, it obviously merited his own attention, in light of the investigation underway.

I'm the man you're looking for. I killed those women with my trusty survival knife, then dumped it. If you want to talk, I'm ready. —Blue Ridge Parkway Killer

Garrett felt a chill at the casualness of the text message from a purported killer. Was this truly their unsub? Had guilt eaten at him like an insidious cancer so he was ready to turn himself in and atone for his crimes through the judicial system? Identifying himself as Special Agent Sneed, he texted the person back, asking for more details. The suspect responded with another text.

All I can tell you right now is I stabbed them multiple times after catching them off guard. The park ranger put up more of a fight but still ultimately succumbed to my blade like the first victim before I ran off into the woods. I'm being straight with you.

Garrett sipped on coffee thoughtfully. *Sounds like someone who was actually involved in the homicides and needed to get this off his chest,* he mused, while still remaining skeptical. Was this simply an attention-seeker who was merely repeating public information or the real deal? If this was indeed their unsub, he was likely using a burner phone to avoid being traced back to his location. They needed to bring him in to further check out or dismiss his story. Garrett asked the man for his name.

You can call me Sean.

Garrett suspected it wasn't his real name, but it was a start in establishing a dialogue. He texted Sean for a face-to-face meeting, expecting him to reject this out of hand. Instead, Garrett was shocked at what came next.

I'm ready to turn myself in, Agent Sneed. Just tell me when and where.

Not willing to look a gift horse in the mouth, in case this was their serial killer, Garrett put him to the test by asking that he report to the Transylvania County Sheriff's Office at noon. When Sean agreed, Garrett immediately phoned Ray Pottenger and informed him that the person of interest in the case was reportedly set to arrive his way in an hour.

Pottenger made arrangements to that effect, accordingly. "We'll see if he shows."

"I'll be there, if he does," Garrett assured him.

He then called Madison. "Hey."

"Hey." He could tell that she was driving and had him on speaker phone.

"Got some news." Garrett told her about Sean using the tip line and the noon meeting at the Transylvania County Sheriff's Office.

"Hmm. You really think this guy is legit?"

"We'll find out soon enough," he responded noncommittally. "He seems to know things."

"Such as?"

"Basic info on the killings that may or may not be a firsthand account."

"I'd like to be there for the interrogation, if it happens," Madison said.

"I want that too," Garrett told her, believing she deserved that much, if they were to make an arrest.

"Good."

"I'll see you then."

"Okay," she replied and left it at that.

After disconnecting, Garrett was pensive. Part of him regretted not spending last night with her. It had been a judgment call. As much as they clicked in bed, he didn't want to overplay his hand in putting more emphasis on the mind-blowing sex than the overall strength of what they had going for them. If things went as they should, there would be plenty of times ahead for much more intimacy between them. Right now, they needed to see if the unsub in the investigation had come to them, rather than the other way around.

THE SUSPECT IDENTIFIED himself as Vincent Sean Deidrick. Madison, who sat beside Garrett, studied the man sitting across from them in the interrogation room. Wearing loose casual attire, he was in his midthirties, slender and around six feet, she guessed. His medium-length black hair was in a bro-flow cut, and he had a chinstrap beard on a long face with a jutting chin. He stared back at her so fiercely with dark eyes, it caused her to turn away briefly before meeting his gaze head-on.

Garrett, who was recording the interview, had the suspect reiterate his name and state his age of thirty-four before asking him straightforwardly, "So, to be sure, Mr. Deidrick, you're confessing to the murders of Olivia Forlani and Nicole Wallenberg?"

"Yeah, I am." His voice did not waver as he lifted the glass of water before him with his right hand and took a sip. "I stabbed them both to death and had no problem doing it."

Garrett drew a breath. "Let's talk about that." He leaned forward. "What exactly did you use to stab the victims?"

"A survival knife," he claimed.

"Can you describe the knife?"

Deidrick shrugged. "Yeah. The blade was eight inches long. Bought it at a hardware store some time ago."

"What type of handle did it have?" Madison thought to ask.

"Just a handle," he said flippantly.

"Well, was it wooden, rubber, what?" she questioned.

He paused. "Rubber, I think."

You think? Or was that a lucky guess? Madison wondered, glancing at Garrett. "So you used the same knife to kill both women?"

"Yeah, it saved me the trouble of having to use different knives." Deidrick gave her a smug look.

Garrett peered at him. "What did you do with the knife?"

"Got rid of it," he replied, taking a drink of the water.

"Got rid of it where?"

"I tossed it in a dumpster."

"Where was that?" Garrett's voice hardened.

"On the parkway somewhere," Deidrick said tonelessly. "In trying to get away, I didn't exactly take the time to keep track of my every move."

"Maybe you should have, now that you're confessing to the murders," Madison stated, her lips pursed with doubts.

He sneered. "Guess I screwed up, huh?"

Garrett angled his face at him. "What about the clothing you were wearing during the murders? I assume you got rid of them, too, since they had to have been covered with your victims' blood."

Deidrick hedged. "Yeah, I did."

"You tossed those in the dumpster too?" Garrett asked.

Deidrick waited a beat and said, "Actually, I washed the clothes. No reason to throw away something I could still wear, right?"

Caught him in at least one lie, Madison thought. How many more lies were there in his story? "Speaking of clothes, do you happen to remember what the victims were wearing when you killed them?" she asked him.

Deidrick squirmed in the chair. "To tell you the truth, I wasn't paying much attention to their clothes." He paused. "The ranger had on a ranger uniform."

Good deduction, Madison mused sardonically. It didn't sound like the voice of direct experience to her. "Tell us again how you went about killing the women and when each killing occurred." She was intent on breaking down his confession even more.

The suspect recounted what he had already said and was able to provide the correct dates and general time frame in which the murders took place. Madison was still not convinced that he was their killer. She exchanged looks with Garrett, who asked him bluntly, "Why did you kill them?"

Deidrick sat back and responded shakily, "A voice in my head told me to do it. Can't really explain, other than to say it was just something I felt compelled to do."

"Why those women in particular?" Madison asked him straightforwardly, wondering if he'd been stalking them beforehand, were he the true culprit.

"They just happened to be in the vicinity when the desire to kill hit me." He regarded her darkly. "Wish it had been you that I came upon instead, Ranger Lynley," he said icily.

Garrett looked as if he was ready to go after him right then and there. "That wouldn't have gone well for you, Deidrick," he stated. "She would have made you work even harder to get what you wanted out of it."

Madison touched Garrett's forearm to let him know that she wasn't flustered by the suspect's attempt at intimidation. "But it wasn't me," she snapped. "I'm here right now, and if you did what you claim to have done, you'll never hurt another woman again."

Deidrick furrowed his brow. "I did it," he insisted. "Killed them both."

"So you say," Garrett muttered. "Why confess now?"

"Why not?" His voice lowered an octave. "I felt

I needed to before the urge to go after someone else overcame me."

"I see." Garrett gave him a quizzical gaze.

"Are you going to arrest me, or what?" he demanded.

Garrett considered the question and said equably, "First, we'd like to collect a sample of your DNA, as well as get your fingerprints, as part of the process."

Deidrick stared at him, nonplussed, and said flatly, "That won't happen till I'm charged with the murders."

As Madison exchanged glances with Garrett in assessing the situation, she took note of Deidrick finishing off his glass of water in practically a show of defiance. She looked up as the door opened and Deputy Pottenger popped his head in. He indicated a need to speak with them outside the room.

"Will you excuse us?" she told Deidrick politely as she stood with Garrett and left him at the table. She wondered what the deputy had for them.

IN THE HALL, Garrett was curious as to what Ray Pottenger had learned after checking out the suspect's background. It was obvious there were some major gaps in Deidrick's account of the killings, which Madison had clearly picked up on as well. That left a lot to be desired in believing him to be the actual Blue Ridge Parkway Killer.

Pottenger scratched his pate and said sourly, "Looks like Vincent Sean Deidrick has had mental health issues most of his life. He's been in and out of institutions and is apparently prone to delusions, among other conditions." The deputy sighed. "Deidrick also happens to be a true-crime addict. Combine these with the fact that most of the accurate information he gave was readily available through the media and online and his story starts to fall apart."

"Why am I not surprised?" Madison frowned. "Deidrick acted like a wannabe serial killer, and now we know why."

"He must have been following the story as it happened," Garrett decided, "and figured this was a good time to make his move for fifteen seconds of notoriety."

Pottenger nodded. "Seems to be the size of it."

"Still, he knew just enough to keep him on the radar," Garrett said. "At least till we're certain that his palm print isn't a match for the one Forensics pulled off the survival knife used in the killings."

"We'll assign a deputy to keep an eye on Deidrick for the time being," Pottenger said.

On that note, Garrett stepped back inside the interrogation room and said disingenuously, "We appreciate you coming in with the confession, Sean. We'll take everything you said under consideration. For now, you're free to go."

Deidrick's nostrils flared. "So, that's it?" he voiced with disappointment. "You're not taking me into custody?"

"Not yet." Garrett jutted his chin. "We can't just go on a confession alone, convincing as it is. There's a process we need to go through. But we have your

address and cell phone number. As soon as everything is in order, we'll bring you back in and go from
there. In the meantime, a deputy will show you out."

Reluctantly, Deidrick got to his feet, and Pottenger
came in and walked him from the room and to the
front door of the sheriff's office. Garrett watched
briefly before going back into the interrogation room,
where he put on a nitrile glove and carefully lifted
the glass Deidrick had drank out of. There was a
clear palm print that he'd left. Garrett put the glass
into an evidence bag. They would get this over to the
Western Regional Crime Laboratory pronto and see
if they had a match.

In Garrett's mind, he doubted that would be the
case. As much as he wanted Vincent Sean Deidrick
to have handed them the guilty party on a silver
platter, it was looking like another red herring in
the effort to bring the cagey Blue Ridge Parkway
Killer to justice.

Chapter Twelve

An hour later, Madison was in her patrol car on the Blue Ridge Parkway, pondering what to make of Vincent Sean Deidrick's confession. She found it hard to imagine that anyone could be so fixated on violent behavior so as to wish to become a serial killer for the vicarious thrill of it. On the other hand, if by some miracle Deidrick did turn out to be the parkway killer, then he had done them a solid by turning himself in.

At least we'd have no trouble tracking him down and bringing him back in with a deputy shadowing his every move, Madison mused.

When her cell phone rang, she put it on speaker after seeing that the caller was Garrett. He had left the sheriff's office to go directly to the crime lab to have the glass Deidrick had drunk from tested for his palm print.

"Hey," she uttered. "What did you find out?"

"That Deidrick's right-hand palm print was not a match for the print left on the survival knife murder weapon," Garrett replied matter-of-factly. "Jewel

Yasumori dismissed any notion that Deidrick might still somehow be our serial killer."

"Figures," she said acceptingly.

"That's the way it works out sometimes in this business. You're going to get people who want to involve themselves in criminal activity, whether real or not. Mix that in with mental issues and you get a Vincent Sean Deidrick."

"I suppose." Madison paused. "Someone knows something," she declared. "Maybe the tip line can still work in terms of providing solid info."

"That may be the case," Garrett said. "Especially with the reward being offered."

"We'll see about that," she told him, though not holding her breath. Cash incentive could only go so far in motivating people to do the right thing. Then there was the real possibility that the killer was hidden in plain view, completely fooling those around him into believing him to be a law-abiding citizen.

"I'm on my way back to the parkway," he told her. "Should be there in about fifteen minutes. Can you meet me at the Raven Rocks Overlook?"

"Yes. Why?" she wondered.

"You'll see…" He left her hanging with his mysterious words, while arousing her curiosity.

"I'll meet you there," Madison told him simply. She drove to the overlook that was popular for its sunsets and rock climbers. After pulling into the parking area, she got out of her car and waited for Garrett's arrival, while enjoying the amazing views of the landscape.

I never tire of this part of working in the Blue Ridge Mountains, she told herself, while knowing that someone was attempting to mar its beauty with ugly acts of criminality.

When Garrett drove up, parking alongside her, Madison headed to meet him. She wondered if he had news pertaining to the investigation. "Hey," she said.

"Hey." He flashed a quick smile, replaced by a serious look. "Thanks for coming."

She blinked and considered that this could be a romantic move on his part. Or not. "What's up?"

"I wanted to show you something." He took her hand and led her to the wooden fence at the edge of the Raven Rocks Overlook. "This is where my mother was murdered," Garrett muttered, maudlin.

Clutching his hand tighter, Madison expressed sympathy as though it had just happened. "I'm so sorry."

"It was down there, where she ventured off a hiking trail." He drew a breath. "Someone was waiting for her or followed her to that spot."

Madison was speechless, unsure what to say. Reliving the memory of his mother's death, still an unsolved mystery, had to be gut-wrenching. Even after all these years. She knew that this had been triggered by the current parkway murders.

I need to try to ease his painful memories, she thought. "Your mother must have been a remarkable woman to have raised you alone, by and large, and still found the time to do something she loved."

"Yeah, she was." Garrett was still holding Madison's hand while staring out at the scenery. Suddenly, he faced her and said, "How do you feel about making our way down there?"

She glanced down. Though it looked a bit tricky, she was sure she could do it without making a fool of herself. Especially if it could help give him some closure. "I'm game if you are." She looked at him. "You sure you want to do this?"

"I'm sure," he said resolutely. "I need to."

They climbed over the fence and headed down the slope across rocks and dirt. At one point, Madison nearly slipped. Catching her in his sturdy arms, Garrett said coolly, "Watch your step."

With a giggle, while regaining her footing, she responded lightheartedly, "Now you tell me."

He chuckled. "You're doing fine."

There were no more hiccups before they reached the lower level that had grass, a dirt path with a wooded area and a thirteen-acre family farm nearby. Madison followed Garrett into the woods and watched as he surveyed the area, as if looking for clues of a three-decades-old homicide.

"She never had a chance once ambushed," he remarked. "Just like Olivia and Nicole."

Madison gazed at him. "You don't think the murders could somehow be connected, do you?"

Garrett pursed his lips thoughtfully. "Anything's possible." He added, "Right now, my mother's murder is still a cold case. The recent murders are heating up, in spite of the setbacks in identifying the unsub."

Madison pondered the possibility that the same killer could have spanned thirty years. Her brother Scott was a cold-case investigator and had cracked some previously unsolved homicides. But in most of these, the killer had laid low through the years. Could this be different?

Garrett got her attention. "After my grandparents' deaths, I kind of turned away from my people in the Eastern Band of Cherokee Indians," he remarked, a tone of guilt in his voice. "Part of me blamed them for not doing more to protect my mother—like getting someone to hike with her in the Blue Ridge Mountains instead of her going alone."

"Do you really think that was fair?" Madison questioned. "Maybe back then it wasn't any more unusual than now for a woman to hike by herself. Especially in this area that's usually considered a safe environment. I'm sure your mom had taken the trek alone other times with no problems."

"She had," he acknowledged, "and you're right." Garrett looked down. "I need to go back to the Qualla, where I still have a few distant relatives and the overall support of the Cherokee community, and make peace with the past and present."

Madison smiled. "That's a great idea."

"How do you feel about taking a ride with me to Cherokee?" he asked.

She knew that this was the tribal capital of the Eastern Band of Cherokee Indians, federally recognized as such, and located at the southern boundary of the Blue Ridge Parkway, around an hour-and-a-

half drive. This would be the first time she had accompanied Garrett to his native land, as he'd been in
no hurry to do so when they'd dated previously—and
now she knew why. Madison had no problem taking
the afternoon off and didn't think her boss would object, with other rangers on hand.

"I'd love to go to Cherokee with you," she told
Garrett.

"Great."

With a grin on his face, he pulled her up to him,
and they kissed. Madison welcomed this show of
affection, the nearness of him causing her heart to
flutter. She hoped that visiting the Qualla would be
just what they needed to bring them closer together.

GARRETT FOLLOWED MADISON back to her place, where
she changed into leisure clothes and put her hair into
a high ponytail and joined him for the drive. There
was silence mostly as they headed down the Great
Smoky Mountains Expressway toward Cherokee in
Jackson County where, along with Haywood and
Swain Counties, the greatest contiguous part of the
Qualla Boundary existed. Purchased by the Native
American tribe in the 1870s and held in trust by the
federal government as a sovereign nation that included forests, rivers and mountains, with the Great
Smoky Mountains National Park nearby, it was a
place that would always be near and dear to Garrett's
heart. Having spent his youth there and embracing
the heritage handed down to him by his mother and
grandparents, it had never been his intention to turn

his back on the Qualla. But it had taken him this long to overcome the self-guilt and blame that had kept him away. He knew now that it had been wrong to put his mother's murder on anyone but the unsub, who had used his own free will to butcher her to death and had gotten away with it.

"So, who are these distant relatives of yours living in the Qualla?" Madison broke the silence from the passenger seat. "And have you kept in touch at all?"

Garrett loosened his grip on the steering wheel as he responded contemplatively, "I've stayed in touch with a second cousin, Noah Owl, and his wife, Breanna. And one of the elders who knew my mother and grandparents, Jeremiah Youngdeer. But that's about it."

"Well, hopefully, this will give you the opportunity to reconnect and start a new chapter in your life as a member of the EBCI," she said.

Garrett grinned. "I'm counting on that." But he was counting even more on strengthening their own reconnection, which could ultimately extend to his greater ties to the Qualla as well as her family.

When they arrived in Cherokee, Garrett drove to a residence on Black Rock Road. A red GMC Yukon was parked outside the rustic log cabin. Before they reached the door, it opened. A yellow Labrador retriever scooted out past them, followed by a tall and firm man in his late thirties with long dark hair parted on the side and deep brown eyes.

He broke into a grin and said, "Hey, stranger."

"Noah." Garrett met his gaze warmly. "Good to see you."

"You too." They embraced, and Noah shifted his eyes. "And who did you bring with you?"

"This is Madison Lynley," Garrett introduced her. "My cousin Noah Owl, who also happens to be the interim chief of the Cherokee Indian Police Department for the EBCI."

"Nice to meet you," Madison said with a smile and extended her hand.

"You too." Noah ignored her hand and gave her a brief hug. "Handshakes are strictly forbidden in these parts."

She laughed. "I'll try to remember that."

He called to the dog, "Bo, get over here!" The yellow Lab immediately bounded over to them on command, and Noah said, "Say hello to our guests."

The dog barked, and Garrett played with him a bit and said, "Good to see you again too," before Bo moved over to Madison, warming up to her instantly.

"Hi, Bo," she said spiritedly.

"What's all the ruckus out here?" a female voice asked.

Garrett turned to see Noah's wife, Breanna, step out. In her midthirties, petite and attractive with big gray-brown eyes and long and layered brunette hair with highlights, she was noticeably pregnant with what would be the couple's first child. Garrett was envious of them and looked forward to the day when he would become a father, along with a husband. "Hey, Breanna."

"Hey, Garrett." She flashed her teeth, hugged him and went to Madison, hugging her before saying,

"You must be Madison, the ranger Garrett has been raving about reconnecting with."

Madison blushed, glancing at him and back. "Yep, that would be me."

"Nice to finally meet you."

"Same here."

Garrett regretted not having brought Madison there for a visit when they'd been seeing each other two years ago. But the timing had been off and he hadn't been in much of a hurry back then to return to Cherokee. He was glad to have her there now as part of his way of mending fences.

"Come inside," Noah told them.

Half an hour later, they were all sitting in rocker chairs on a wraparound deck with an amazing view of the Blue Ridge Parkway and the mountains. They talked about the parkway killings, life on the Qualla, which had seen an increase in drug activity in recent memory, and spending more time together. Garrett was certainly amenable to getting in touch with his roots again, with Madison being an essential part of that in bridging the gap, while looking ahead.

"So, how close are you to discovering who's behind the murders on the parkway?" Breanna asked, sipping lemonade.

Garrett furrowed his brow and glanced at Bo, who was lying there lazily, taking it all in. "Not close enough to say that an arrest is imminent," he admitted. "But we're doing everything we can to track down the culprit."

Madison concurred. "It's a work in progress," she asserted positively, "frustrating as it's been."

Breanna sighed. "Just keep at it, and you'll get some justice."

"That's the plan," he said, his voice intent.

Noah drank some beer and said, "This has to hit pretty close to home, losing your mother in a similar fashion?"

"It does," Garrett acknowledged. This was one reason for his return, to try to reconcile what had happened to her with the current murders. "I kind of feel that she's pushing me to get to the bottom of the current investigation as a way to make amends for the past."

"None of what happened thirty years ago was your fault," Noah told him. "You get that, right?"

"Yeah," he said tonelessly, taking a swig of beer. "But there's still a side of me that wishes I had gone with her that day to the Blue Ridge Mountains. Maybe if I had, we would've taken a different route and she wouldn't have run into harm's way."

"Coulda, woulda, shoulda," Noah voiced in rejecting the idea. "We all go when our time's up, like it or not. That wasn't your time, Garrett, and you weren't in a position then to change fate. Don't beat yourself up in reliving a tragedy that was beyond your control."

"I feel the same way," Madison expressed gently, sipping beer. "Losing loved ones is the hardest thing. Worse would be to tarnish their memories by dwelling too much on the what-ifs."

"You're right." Garrett nodded in agreement, happy to have her in his corner. But even with that understanding, there was still something that wasn't sitting right with him between his mother's murder and the current ones attributed to the Blue Ridge Parkway Killer. Was it even possible after all these years that the killer could be one and the same?

BEFORE THEY LEFT, Garrett paid a courtesy call to Jeremiah Youngdeer, who was on the Tribal Council. At eighty, he was still rock solid in build and had short silver hair and black eyes deeply creased at the corners. As a Cherokee elder, he carried the respect afforded to him among the Eastern Band of Cherokee Indians.

"Nice to be back here," Garrett told him as they walked through the Oconaluftee Indian Village, an authentic replica of a 1760s Cherokee village, on Drama Road.

"You're always welcome, Garrett," Jeremiah told him, walking with a limp from arthritis in his knee. "This is your home too, no matter where you go in life."

Garrett smiled respectfully. "I appreciate that."

Jeremiah regarded him. "I want you to know that not a day goes by that I don't think about your mother, Jessica," he said, maudlin. "As one of our own, we all felt incredible pain over the unfortunate loss of life for her at such a young age."

Garrett waited a beat before asking in a low voice, "Do you remember my father, Andrew Crowe?"

"I do." Jeremiah's weathered face sagged. "Andrew was a hard worker. Sadly, he also developed a predilection for the bottle. It caused him to forget a big part of his heritage and commitment to family." He took a deep breath. "Your mother wanted to stay with him, become his wife. But by then, Andrew was too far gone, and he left her—and his people—high and dry. And that was it. He never returned to the Qualla."

Garrett got a lump in his throat at the thought of being cheated out of having a real father. Especially in light of his mother's early death. But since Andrew Crowe had made his choice, it was something Garrett would have to live with, as he had all these years, while maintaining strength through his mother's memory.

He eyed Jeremiah, knowing what would come next was delicate but necessary. "Is it possible that someone from the Qualla could have followed my mother to the mountains and killed her?" Given that his father had abandoned them two years prior for parts unknown, Garrett had no reason to believe that he had perpetrated the attack as domestic violence.

The elder creased his brow. After a long moment, he responded levelly, "Anything is possible. But with my ear to the ground then and the strong sense of community, I'm all but certain that it was someone from the outside who randomly crossed paths with Jessica and decided to harm her."

Garrett nodded. This was his sense too. Which gave him peace of mind on the one hand. And on the other, a renewed sense that his mother's killer might not only still be alive and well but could have picked up where he'd left off years ago in hunting young women in the Blue Ridge Mountains.

MADISON WAS HAPPY that Garrett had invited her to accompany him to the Qualla Boundary and get to know his relatives and the richness of the environment itself. They were able to step away from the pressures of the criminal investigation by hanging out at Harrah's Cherokee Casino and going to a fun Cherokee bonfire, where they listened to amazing stories by Cherokees told to the sound of drums.

When they got back, Madison spent the night at Garrett's log cabin. Putting aside any hesitancy to fall back into enjoyable old and recent habits, they made love, enjoying each other's company while extending their passions well into the wee hours of the morning. Afterward, thoroughly exhausted, they lay cuddled together in his log bed, where Madison could have sworn that Garrett said he loved her before drifting off to sleep. She wondered if this had been a slip of the tongue in the aftermath of good sex. Or had he meant it?

Given that her own feelings for the man had risen to the "starting to fall in love" category since they had become involved again, Madison could only hope that this was indeed reciprocal as they navigated the waters of a renewed romance that came with the same risks and rewards as before. Only this time would hurt far worse should things fizzle out and they ended up going their separate ways. She fell asleep on that note, while resolved to remain positive where Garrett Sneed was concerned.

Chapter Thirteen

"I'd like to take a look at the cold-case file on my mother's unsolved murder," Garrett told his boss in a video chat the following day at the cabin.

"Really?" Carly Tafoya raised a brow in surprise. "Do you think it has something to do with the parkway murders?"

He considered the question carefully, knowing full well that this was a long shot at best and a waste of precious time at worst. Nevertheless, it was a shot that he needed to pursue. "There are some similarities that simply can't be ignored," Garrett reasoned. "For one, they occurred in the Blue Ridge Mountains, albeit thirty years apart. The female victims were all stabbed to death," he pointed out uneasily. "With none of the various suspects for the two recent murders panning out, I decided I needed to expand the range of possible unsubs to include those old enough to have murdered my mother."

Carly gave an understanding nod. "Okay, I'll send you what we have on the case."

Garrett smiled. "Thanks."

"You might also check with the Buncombe County Sheriff's Office," she suggested. "They would have been the local law enforcement agency to head the investigation in working in conjunction with us."

"I'll do that." He was sure he would get cooperation from Sheriff Jacob Silva. "Can you look up the name of the special agent who handled my mother's case?"

"Yes. Give me a sec." Carly stepped away for a moment. She said when returning, "It was Special Agent Dexter Broderick. He retired about fifteen years ago and is still alive."

That's good to know, Garrett thought. "I don't suppose you know his whereabouts?"

"As a matter of fact, he lives in Buncombe County," she told him. "At least that was his last known address."

"Send me his contact info. Hopefully I can track him down."

"Will do." Carly paused. "Honestly, Sneed, linking these cases seems like a stretch, as the culprit in your mother's murder would have to be pretty old today and likely not as able-bodied as a younger man to commit two brazen murders on the parkway and make a clean getaway in the woods in a snap. I'm just saying. Don't want to see you get too keen on the prospect of solving your mother's murder, only to be left disappointed."

This was fair to point out to Garrett, leaving him little room for push back. Especially as these were legitimate points in his own mind too, all things considered. But his gut told him that, even against the odds, he might be onto something. "I appreciate your concern," he voiced evenly. "If at any time it seems like I'm barking up the wrong tree, I won't reopen a cold case that doesn't appear to be connected to my present investigation," he promised. "I'm totally committed to solving the deaths of Nicole Wallenberg and Olivia Forlani, no matter what it takes."

"Okay," Carly said acceptingly.

After signing off, for an instant, Garrett had second thoughts about going down this road. Did he really want to dredge up old and painful memories at a time when he had just started to get back in touch with his roots? Then he realized it was for that very reason that he needed to see this through, for better or worse.

Even Madison seemed to support the possible connection. He had run it by her in the middle of the night, somewhere between the sounds of intimacy and uttering his love for her. She had responded positively on both fronts, giving him reason to believe they were on the same page in terms of the investigation and wanting to be together as a couple when this was all over.

Half an hour later, Garrett was giving the material on his mother's death a cursory glance on his laptop. Jessica Rachel Sneed, age twenty-five, had been found dead below Raven Rocks Overlook on the Blue Ridge Parkway. Fully clothed in a green T-shirt, denim shorts and tennis shoes, she'd been stabbed to death. Next to the body had been a pink lightweight backpack that had contained the victim's water bottle and a few other personal effects. Garrett winced when he read from the autopsy report that his mother had had eight stab wounds to her body. The murder weapon, a survival knife, was shown and described as having a smooth eight-inch, single-edged blade. It had been found by some kids playing in the bushes.

Garrett couldn't help but think that the knife bore a strong resemblance to the one found in a dumpster and positively linked to the murders of Olivia Forlani and Nicole Wallenberg. Was this coincidence? Or an indication that a decades-old killer had a preference for a long-bladed survival knife?

DNA had been collected at the crime scene, including an unknown DNA profile belonging to the unsub that had never been positively identified. Garrett gazed at a photograph of his mother that had been taken earlier that year she'd died. He remembered it being shot by his grandfather outside their house in the Qualla. *She looks so young*, Garrett thought, with her high cheekbones on a diamond-shaped face and bold brown eyes, surrounded by long black hair worn in braids. The resemblance to himself was unmistakable.

He had to check himself at the thought that they had never been given the chance to get to know one another as adults. Hell, his mother hadn't even been around during his teenage years. Or when he'd left the nest in becoming a man and a special agent with the National Park Service. But maybe they could bridge the gap across the spiritual divide should he be able to solve her murder at long last.

Garrett turned to the info on retired Special Agent Dexter Broderick. Now seventy-five, he was apparently residing at a nursing home in Asheville on Mountainly Lane.

Let's see what blanks he can fill in, Garrett thought, and he was out the door.

MADISON RECEIVED A report of a possible armed robbery by Milepost 374.4, close to the Rattlesnake Lodge Trailhead. She headed there to rendezvous with Law Enforcement Ranger Richard Edison.

Back to business as usual...somewhat, she thought, with the Blue Ridge Parkway Killer still on her mind.

Garrett had just called to say that he was en route to see the retired ISB special agent who'd worked on the original Jessica Sneed investigation. Seemed as though Garrett was now of the belief that his mother's death might be tied to the current serial murders on the parkway. The notion gave Madison a fright. But it was also something she could see as a possibility, remote as it seemed given the wide time frame.

If Jessica's killer is still at large today, he deserves to be apprehended and sent to prison, Madison told herself. And if the unsub and the present-day perp were one and the same, all the better to solve it in one fell swoop.

Pulling off the parkway behind Richard's vehicle, Madison got out and approached him as he spoke to a thirtysomething Asian man standing beside his car, a blue BMW Gran Coupe.

Richard turned to her. "Hey."

"What happened?" she asked, looking from one to the other.

"This is Pierre Yang," Richard said. "Why don't you tell Ranger Lynley what you told me?"

Madison gazed at the brown-eyed man, who was medium in build with short dark hair in a spiky cut, as he told her, "I pulled off to the side here to take some pics, and another car stopped. A guy got out, carrying a gun, and demanded my cell phone, camera and wallet, which had cash and credit cards in it." His voice shook. "Of course, I gave them to him. He got back in his vehicle and took off. I had a second phone in my car that I used to call you guys."

She frowned. "Sorry you had to go through that, sir."

"Me too." He scratched his pate. "Guess I shouldn't have stopped here."

"You have every right to." Madison believed that the culprit had likely followed the mark and waited for an opportunity to strike, as was the case for these types of crimes. She faced Richard. "Did you get a description of the suspect?"

"Yeah." He glanced at a notepad. "White male in his teens. Slender, blue-eyed with blondish-brown hair in a fringe cut and wearing a white T-shirt, jeans and black sneakers." Richard looked at the victim. "Is that right?"

"Yes," Pierre replied with a nod.

"What type of car was he driving?" Madison asked. She listened as he described it as a dark-colored sedan similar to a Mitsubishi Eclipse. When asked about the weapon the unsub was brandishing, Pierre believed it to be a .22 caliber pistol. "We'll do what we can to help you retrieve some of your stolen items," she told him. "I would strongly suggest you cancel the credit cards right away, to limit your liability."

"I'll do that," he assured her.

"Good." Madison turned to Richard and said, "After you finish taking Mr. Yang's statement, notify the local authorities and see if they have reports of any similar crimes of late. Could be this is part of a theft ring, seizing upon any opportunities that come their way on the parkway or greater area."

"Okay." Richard adjusted his campaign hat and looked at Pierre. "Let's go over everything that happened."

Madison left them, knowing that her fellow law enforcement ranger could take it from here. She headed back to her patrol vehicle, wondering why so many teenagers seemed to be going off the rails these days. She supposed there could be many explanations, not the least of which was a misguided belief that they were owed something for nothing. If she were so fortunate to have children of her own someday, she would certainly do her best to ensure they were well grounded with strong values. Madison couldn't help but think that if their father happened to be Garrett, he would be of the same mind.

GARRETT PULLED INTO the parking area of the Seniors at Blue Ridge Retirement Village. He got out and went inside the Victorian-style facility. At the front desk, he flashed his identification and asked to see Dexter Broderick. A moment later, a fortysomething female with a platinum bouffant approached him in the lobby and said, "I'm Wendy Schneider, the nursing home manager and health services coordinator."

"Special Agent Sneed," he told her.

"You wanted to speak with Mr. Broderick?"

"Yes. I'm looking into a cold case he investigated when he was with the National Park Service."

Wendy arched a brow. "Not sure he can be much help to you, Agent Sneed," she indicated sadly. "Mr. Broderick is currently suffering from moderate dementia as a result of Alzheimer's disease. His memory loss is pretty significant, and he's easily confused."

"Sorry to hear that." Garrett had come across people with Alzheimer's in his personal and professional life and wouldn't wish this progressive disease on anyone.

"But there are times when he's lucid," she said. "Moreover, Mr. Broderick rarely gets any visitors these days. He's currently out in the garden getting some fresh air. You're welcome to speak with him for a few minutes, if you like."

"I would like to do that, thanks," Garrett said, believing it was worth a try.

He was led through the facility and out a door to a large area with a well-manicured lawn, a variety of plants and flowers, a wilderness path and a pond.

They approached an elderly, thin man who was sitting on an Adirondack rocking chair in a shaded area.

"Mr. Broderick," Wendy got his attention. "There's someone here to see you."

"Really?" Dexter's blue eyes lit beneath thinning white hair in a Boston style with a widow's peak.

"I'm Special Agent Garrett Sneed," Garrett said and stuck out his hand. Reluctantly, Dexter shook it with his own frail hand. "You worked on a case for the National Park Service thirty years ago."

"Did I?" He scratched his pate in straining to remember.

"It was a murder investigation on the Blue Ridge Parkway." Garrett took a breath. "The victim, Jessica Sneed, was my mother."

"Jessica Sneed?" Dexter's chin sagged. "Your mother?"

"That's right. I've reopened the case in trying to solve the crime," Garrett told him. "She was stabbed to death." He glanced at Wendy, who had stepped farther away to give them a little privacy but was clearly listening to every word, based on her expression.

"I'm sorry," the older man said sincerely. "I tried to find out who did it."

"I know you did." Garrett was thankful for his service and that his memory was still there on this occasion. "Do you recall anything that might be able to help me find her killer?"

Dexter sucked in a deep breath, peered at him and said, "Who did you say you are?"

"Special Agent Sneed of the National Park Service."

Dexter's eyes narrowed suspiciously. "Do I know you?"

"We just met." Garrett could see that he was losing him. "We were talking about the murder of Jessica Sneed on the Blue Ridge Parkway."

"We were?" Dexter widened his eyes, but they looked blank. "Sorry, but my memory isn't what it used to be. What is this about? And who did you say you are?"

Guess this is about as far as I'm going to get, Garrett thought, eyeing Wendy as her cue that the interview was over. He turned back to the former special agent and said, "Just a friend who came to check on you."

Dexter looked confused, then broke into a grin. "Nice of you. Thanks."

"Anytime." Garrett forced a smile. "Take care of yourself, Dexter."

"I will."

Wendy walked up to them and said to Garrett, "Hope you don't feel this was a waste of your time."

"I don't," he stressed. "NPS special agents always have a bond, no matter what. I'll show myself out."

Maybe I'll have better luck at the Buncombe County Sheriff's Office, Garrett told himself as he took the short drive there. That was assuming this wasn't a wild goose chase in trying to open a cold case by tying it to a current investigation.

When he arrived, Sheriff Jacob Silva greeted him and said, "I had one of my deputies pull up what we had on the Jessica Sneed case and lay it out in an evidence room for you to take a look at."

"Appreciate that," Garrett told him.

"No problem." Silva furrowed his brow. "I warn you, though, it may be difficult to look at."

"I get that." Garrett met his eyes steadily. "I'm up to the task."

"All right." Silva lifted the brim of his hat. "If we can do anything else to help solve your mother's murder, we're more than willing to do so."

"Thanks. I'll let you know."

Silva gave him a thoughtful look. "You're thinking that the same killer could now be targeting women on the parkway?"

Garrett waited a beat before responding contemplatively, "All options are on the table at this point."

"They should be." The sheriff bobbed his head. "Some of the worst serial killers started early in life and stayed at it or picked back up in their later years."

Garrett kept that thought in mind as he walked into the evidence room. On the metal rectangular table was a pair of nitrile gloves and evidence collected from the crime scene on the parkway thirty years ago. In plastic bags were his mother's clothing, shoes and backpack. Also bagged was the murder weapon. He put on the gloves and opened the bag, examining the survival knife while holding it by the wooden handle. This differentiated from the rubber handle used in the stabbing deaths of Olivia Forlani and Nicole Wallenberg. He didn't put much stock in that, as different times, different handles.

Garrett swallowed hard as he put the knife back into the bag, pained at what it had done to his mother. Had the same unsub used another knife to resume murdering women? Or was the case unrelated, if not just as sickening? Once he had perused the evidence and gone over some witness statements and incidental notes by investigators, Garrett had seen enough to warrant continuing to investigate what could well have been a one-off in the killing of his mother.

Outside the room, he spoke with Sheriff Silva, who pledged continued cooperation and added, "By the way, the sheriff thirty years ago, Lou Buckley, is now retired and living the good life in Kiki's Ridge. You might want to speak with him. I'm sure he'd be happy to tell you what he remembers about the case."

"I'll do that," Garrett said, more than willing to follow up on this with the former sheriff in the pursuit of long overdue justice.

Chapter Fourteen

That afternoon, Madison accompanied Garrett to Price Lake at Milepost 297, where they found the man they were looking for, she believed. Retired Buncombe County Sheriff Lou Buckley was standing on the pier, trout fishing. It saddened her to learn that his former colleague in law enforcement, retired ISB Special Agent Dexter Broderick, was suffering from Alzheimer's disease. Madison recalled that her grandfather had been in the early stages of dementia before eventually dying from a heart attack.

"Since Buckley's office had jurisdiction on the homicide at that time, hopefully he can provide some insight into the case," Garrett told her as they walked down the long pier.

"We'll see," she said, still wrapping her mind around the notion that a cold case could be the key to solving a current one. She wondered if the unsub was the same or if they were connected to one another in some way.

Garrett cut into her reverie, remarking, "Glad to hear that your teenage armed robber ran out of steam quickly."

"That's what happens when you're dumb enough to try to use a stolen credit card less than an hour after stealing it." She rolled her eyes at the stupidity of the young criminal. "Duh."

He laughed. "Well, thieves aren't always the brightest bulbs in the chandelier."

"I'm just happy for the victim that his items were recovered with minimal loss," she said, while knowing Pierre Yang's story could have ended much more tragically since he was robbed at gunpoint.

"Yeah." They approached the seventysomething man, who was heavyset and wearing a fishing trucker hat with tufts of white hair beneath it. Garrett asked, "Sheriff Lou Buckley?"

He turned to face them with blue eyes behind browline glasses. "Haven't been called that in a very long time."

"Once a sheriff, always a sheriff," Garrett uttered respectfully.

Lou chuckled. "True enough."

"I'm ISB Special Agent Garrett Sneed, and this is Law Enforcement Ranger Madison Lynley."

"Nice to meet you both." He was holding a lightweight trout rod in the water. "In fact, Sheriff Silva gave me a heads up that you wanted to talk to me about a cold case—the murder of Jessica Sneed… your mother."

Garrett nodded. "That's right. I'm reopening the investigation. Anything you can tell us about the case would be helpful."

"First of all, I'm sorry she was killed that way,"

Lou expressed. "I seem to recall that you were, what, about five at the time?"

"Yes," he acknowledged, tilting his face to one side.

Lou glanced out at the lake and back. "Losing your mother at such a young age...you both deserved better." He paused reflectively. "I had just been the sheriff of Buncombe County for a couple of years when the crime occurred on the Blue Ridge Parkway. It threw us all for a loop, as the parkway had been relatively peaceful in those days. Initially, our office battled it out with the National Park Service on who should take the lead in the investigation. Guess I had a stronger will and won out."

Madison asked him curiously, "What takeaways did you get from the case?"

Lou considered this before responding, "The biggest takeaway, I suppose, was that the killer had to have been someone who knew the parkway inside and out. This would have given him a way in and out quickly."

"You mean like a park employee?" Garrett wondered.

"Possibly, though we were able to eliminate as suspects everyone on duty that day. Even off duty workers, for that matter. Unfortunately, we didn't have the same access and inroads to visitors on the parkway or national forest. As such, it was likely someone among this group who killed your mother."

Garrett's jaw set. "Were there any similar murders during that time frame?" He thought about the evidence he'd reviewed in the case.

Lou sighed musingly. "As a matter of fact, a year later, a young woman was stabbed to death in a similar fashion near the Yadkin Valley Overlook on the parkway."

"Was the killer ever caught?" Madison asked.

"Yeah, an arrest was made a couple of days later. Man named Blake O'Donnell confessed to the crime, while insisting he played no part in the murder of Jessica Sneed. Seemed like we had an open-and-shut case." Lou paused, frowning. "Then O'Donnell recanted his confession, claiming it had been coerced. The jury never bought it. Neither did I. He was tried, convicted and sent to prison."

"Was he ever released?" Garrett questioned.

Lou shook his head. "He was killed behind bars, five years into his sentence. Ironically, he was stabbed to death by a fellow inmate after getting into a fight."

Could the jury have gotten it wrong and sent a man to prison for a crime he hadn't committed? Madison couldn't help but ask herself. Might the Blue Ridge Parkway Killer have more murders under his belt than met the eye?

She took a step closer and asked the former sheriff intently, "Do you think it's possible that Jessica's killer could be at it again, killing women on the parkway?" She assumed he was aware of what was happening and the similarities between the cases.

Lou looked out at the lake, where his rod remained

in search of fresh trout. "The unsub would likely be in his fifties and up," he muttered. "As I'm sure you know, most serial killers are younger than that. But the comparisons are hard to ignore. Even for an old geezer like me." He took a breath. "Anything's possible. If this is the direction you're going in, you're welcome to all my files on the original case, which I have in some boxes in my basement. If you'd like, I can send them over to the sheriff's office. Or to the Pisgah Ranger District headquarters. Your call."

"We'd like that," Garrett readily agreed. "The ranger district office would be good."

"Consider it done," he said. "Again, I regret that when I was the Buncombe County Sheriff, we were unable to crack the case of your mother's death. It's one that got away."

"Don't beat yourself up, Sheriff. Not all cases go as we'd like them to." Garrett looked at him sympathetically. "I've had my fair share of investigations that dried up and there was nothing I could do about it."

"Same here," Madison pitched in, wanting to ease his burden, while knowing that law enforcement was anything but a perfect science where all the bad people were held accountable for their actions. Still, she could only hope that the unsub or unsubs who'd left Jessica Sneed, Olivia Forlani and Nicole Wallenberg dead well before their times would one day have to face justice.

"Well, we'll let you get back to your fishing," Garrett told Lou, adding, "I heard that rainbow and brook trout are out in force right now."

"Yeah, they are," he concurred, "along with brown trout and smallmouth bass. If you ever want to join me, be my guests."

Garrett grinned. "We'll keep that in mind."

They walked away from him, and Madison looked at Garrett and said, "I didn't know you were into fishing."

"I grew up fishing in the Qualla," he told her. "Not really my thing these days. But maybe once I'm retired from federal law enforcement, I can take it up again."

"Cool." She tried to picture him in retirement mode. Or herself, for that matter. If they could grow old together, all the better. Was this something he pictured as well? Or were they living in more of a fantasy world right now in being involved romantically again, with reality setting in once the cases before them were put to rest?

As PROMISED, Lou Buckley had his files on the Jessica Sneed cold case delivered late that afternoon to the head office of the Pisgah Ranger District. That evening, Garrett went through them with Madison at her house. They sat at the dining room table poring over the materials while sipping wine, looking for anything that stood out as relevant to the current murders. Admittedly, Garrett wondered if they were searching for a needle in a haystack, given the thirty-year spread since his mother's murder. Had her killer really resurfaced and, as such, was out there for Garrett to find and bring to justice? Or was he deluding himself on a false premise?

I can't shake the feeling that there's something to my intuition, Garrett told himself as he tasted the wine. Maybe her killer had murdered another woman the following year and had been lucky enough to have someone else take the rap, giving the unsub a free pass to kill other women in the years to follow.

He looked at the sketch of an unidentified male that had been reported by witnesses as being on the parkway around the time of his mother's murder. The man was described as being anywhere from his mid-twenties to midthirties and sturdily built with dark eyes and a long nose, while possibly wearing outdoor work clothes. The authorities had never been able to locate the unsub. Garrett recalled Sheriff Buckley stating that park workers had been accounted for and eliminated as suspects. Meaning the unsub had likely worked elsewhere but could still have been a local who'd known the lay of the land. So, who was he and what had become of him? Was this the killer or a false lead?

Garrett gazed at Madison, who was still in uniform but oh so sexy. And, frankly, distracting. She was the one definite positive that had come from his returning to this region to work. Wherever they went from here, he wanted it to be as a couple and all that came with it. When she looked up at him, he considered looking away but couldn't.

She batted her lashes curiously. "What?"

"Nothing," he said, as if she believed him, while he suppressed a grin.

"Right." Madison glanced at the paperwork spread before her and back. "Since I've got your attention, in looking this over and the lists of identified suspects, it seems like the one name that keeps popping up in the notes is Neil Novak. And with good reason. Take a look."

Garrett gazed at a file she handed him and saw the name. Neil Novak, age thirty-four at the time, had been an unemployed wrangler. A partial fingerprint belonging to Novak had been found on the survival knife that'd been used to kill Jessica Sneed. When confronted with this, Novak had claimed that the knife had been stolen a week earlier. As there had been no other physical evidence connecting him to the crime and Novak had had a rock-solid alibi after finding work when the murder had occurred, authorities had had no choice but to eliminate him as a suspect.

"So, maybe Novak never really had his knife stolen and faked the alibi," Madison contended, "and was able to get away with the murder of your mother."

"Hmm…" Garrett chewed on that notion. Alibis could certainly be falsified. It happened more often than people realized. The investigators on the case could only play the hand dealt them. Sometimes they got it wrong. Even when the evidence, or lack thereof, suggested otherwise. "You're right—maybe we do need to take another hard look at Neil Novak, assuming he's still alive."

"I think so," she agreed. "And if Novak is among the living, is he local?"

"He'd be sixty-four now," Garrett pointed out. "Old enough to be out of the killing business, based on official data for the age range of typical killers—but still young enough, per se, to be able to perpetrate murders currently as the Blue Ridge Parkway Killer," he reasoned.

Madison perked up. "It's a lead anyway." She sipped her wine.

"Yeah." He gave her an agreeable look. "I think we need to learn everything we can about Neil Novak and what he may or may not have been up to."

"We will," she said steadfastly. "Wherever the leads take us, right?"

"Right." Garrett held up the sketch of an unsub. "And there's also this person to consider."

Madison grabbed the sketch, studying it. "True. Or he could have been someone's imagination or a male suspect that was totally unrelated to the death of your mother."

"That's possible," Garrett was inclined to agree, while still having to regard him as a person of interest. He drank wine as a thought suddenly entered his head. "Doesn't your brother Scott specialize in cold cases?"

"Yeah." Madison gazed at him. "Why do you ask?"

"Well, given that we've opened one, I thought you could get him on the phone to see if he could give us some input on cold cases in general."

"Really?" She flashed a look of surprise.

He chuckled. "Why not? Might help the cause." *At the very least, it could help me make further inroads in winning points with your family*, Garrett told himself. He assumed that Scott and her other siblings knew by now that they were seeing each other again.

"Okay." Madison got to her feet and grabbed her laptop. She put it on the table and sat next to him. "Sure you want to do this?"

"Of course." He grinned. "I'm not too proud to ask for help."

"Just checking." She smiled and called her brother for a video chat. When Scott accepted it, Madison said cheerfully, "Hey."

Scott smiled. "Hey, sis."

"You remember Garrett?"

"Of course," he said. "Special Agent Sneed. How are you?"

"I'm good." Garrett could read the surprise on his face in wondering what this was all about in reacquainting themselves with one another.

"So, what's up?" Scott asked.

Madison leaned forward and said, "We're looking into the murder of Garrett's mom thirty years ago."

Scott raised a brow. "Oh…?"

"We think it could be tied to a current case we're investigating," Garrett told him equably.

"The Blue Ridge Parkway killings?"

"You've got it," he verified. "Between the similar pattern and a dangerous unsub still at large, it seemed worth exploring the possibility that my mother's killer could be back and targeting other young women on the parkway. Since you specialize in cold cases, we thought you might have some general thoughts about this…"

Before Scott could respond, Madison added, "And according to the sheriff at the time, there was a similar murder that occurred in the county a year later, in which a man confessed and recanted the confession but was still convicted of the crime. There is at least a possibility that he didn't commit the crime and the unsub who killed Jessica Sneed was the real killer, which would still make it a cold case, apart from the present serial killer on the loose."

"Wow," Scott uttered. "That's a lot to unpack."

"Take your time," she quipped.

He chuckled. "Without knowing the details of your mother's case, Garrett, I can tell you that cold cases can be tricky but still resolvable, even without the benefit of the culprit resuming his activities much later down the line."

Garrett listened attentively as Scott ran off some of the dynamics of cold cases that were typically violent and/or gained national attention, citing tunnel vision and advances in forensics as key variables that merited a second look for many such open-ended cases. Having worked on some cold cases in his career, Garrett had been privy to this but was happy to get Scott's take, if only to bridge the familial gap between them for the sake of smoothing the way toward a bright future with Madison.

"Jack the Ripper is obviously one notorious example of a very cold-case killer, who got away with murdering at least five prostitutes in Whitechapel in London's East End in 1888," Scott said. "While the infamous serial killer might never be identified conclusively, other cases and your mother's death could still be solved by identifying the unsub."

"You think?" Garrett asked in all seriousness.

"Yeah. May take some time though," he cautioned. "Not to tell you how to do your job, but you'll need to reexamine evidence, reinterview witnesses, seek out new evidence, etcetera."

"We get the picture," Madison ribbed him.

"You wanted my advice." Scott chuckled. "Anything I can do to help."

"Appreciate that," Garrett said sincerely. "I never turn down any free advice." *Especially coming from one of Madison's siblings*, he mused.

"Neither do I," Scott said and waited a beat. "So, what else is going on with you two? Anything I should know about?"

Garrett deferred to Madison on that one, not wanting to put words in her mouth in sharing his own thoughts on the matter.

Blushing, she told her brother simply, "We're good."

"Fair enough," Scott responded.

"Maybe better than good," Garrett spoke up. "But what do I know?"

Madison laughed and pushed him so he nearly fell off the chair. "Trust your instincts."

Scott laughed. "You heard my sister. Never argue with her. You'll lose every time."

He had to chuckle, though not wanting to ever test that theory any more than he had previously. "I'll keep that in mind."

After they ended the video chat, Madison said curiously, "Still think that was a good idea?"

"Absolutely." Garrett gave her a devilish grin. "Scott helped in more ways than one."

"Really?"

"Yes. He's convinced me that being on your good side always has its benefits."

She showed her teeth tantalizingly. "What might those be?"

"This for one…" Garrett kissed her and, at least for the time being, put aside the cold case he suddenly felt obsessed with thawing.

Chapter Fifteen

The next morning, Garrett gathered all he could on Neil Novak. Turned out that Novak was very much alive and living in Transylvania County. He had also spent time in prison for drug possession early in his life. Though there was no record of him being violence-prone, as far as Garrett was concerned Novak topped the list as a person of interest in his mother's murder.

"Think he'll talk with us?" Madison asked during the drive to visit the suspect.

Garrett sat back behind the steering wheel. "We're not going to give him much of a choice," he declared firmly. "If Novak had anything to do with my mother's murder, he's going to pay for it." Tightening his fingers around the wheel, Garrett added, "Same is true if he's the unsub in the Blue Ridge Parkway homicides."

They arrived at the Novak Ranch, a sprawling property with horses grazing on rolling hills, winding trails and mountain views on Chesterdale Lane in Owen Creek.

"Looks like Novak has done well for himself over the years," Madison commented after they stepped out of the car.

"Looks can be deceiving," Garrett muttered. "Beyond that, it's hard to escape from one's past if there's something there to escape from."

"True enough."

They bypassed the large Craftsman-style home and headed straight for the stables, where they heard voices. Inside, Garrett spotted a tall and slender thirtysomething woman with flaming long and wavy red hair at a stall feeding a quarter horse. Beside her was a sixtysomething man who was taller and heavier, wearing a white wide-brimmed cowboy hat with curly gray hair beneath and sporting a gray ducktail beard.

Garrett overheard the woman refer to the man as "Dad," and she appeared to be concerned about his working too hard. When they heard footsteps approaching, the two turned and stopped talking.

"Are you Neil Novak?" Garrett addressed the man.

"Yep, that's me." He peered at him through dark eyes. "Who's asking?"

"Special Agent Sneed, from the National Park Service's Investigative Services Branch." Garrett flashed his identification. "And this is Law Enforcement Ranger Lynley."

"Hi," Madison spoke evenly to both of them.

Novak jutted his chin. "What's this all about?"

"A cold-case homicide," Garrett responded succinctly.

The woman cocked a brow. "Dad…?"

"I've got this, Dominique." Novak tensed. "I'll see you in the house."

She looked as though she wanted to object, as green eyes darted from Garrett to Madison, before landing back on her father, after which she relented, "All right."

Garrett watched as she walked away, putting some distance between them. He gazed at Novak and said bluntly, "We've reopened the investigation into the murder of Jessica Sneed on the Blue Ridge Parkway." He drew a breath. "She was my mother."

"The parkway killing." Novak scratched his beard nervously. "Sorry that happened to your mother, but that was a long time ago. What does it have to do with me?"

"A survival knife that had your partial fingerprint on it was found to be the murder weapon, Mr. Novak," Madison told him. "I'd say it has everything to do with you."

"As I told the investigators back then, the knife was stolen from my pickup truck. I have no idea who took it and no knowledge of what it was used for by the thief." Novak breathed heavily out his nose. "In any event, I was cleared of any wrongdoing."

"About that," Garrett said. "It seems like your name continued to come up in the investigation in spite of the alibi. Why do you suppose that is?"

"You tell me." Novak's brow creased. "Maybe the cops and rangers thought I was somehow capable of being in two places at once. Well, I wasn't. On the day your mother was killed, I was working on a ranch thirty miles from the parkway and had plenty of others there who could vouch for it. Including the ranch's owner. Now I have my own ranch and have tried to put that dark time behind me for good. Obviously, that isn't so easy for you. Sorry you wasted your time coming here, but I can't help you solve the case."

"Can't?" Garrett glared at him. "Or won't?"

Novak stroked the quarter horse's neck. "Can't," he insisted, his voice steady. "Look, I'm older now and have nothing to hide. If that's all, I have a ranch to run."

Madison lifted her eyes up. "We think that whoever murdered Jessica Sneed may be back at it again," she stated.

His head snapped back. "What are you saying?"

"Two women have been stabbed to death recently on the parkway. The similarities to Ms. Sneed's murder, type of weapon used and location have given us reason to believe that they may have been committed by the same man."

Novak leaned against the stall thoughtfully, tilting the brim of his hat. "Same person thirty years later? Is that even possible?"

"Yes, it's quite possible," Garrett told him. "We think that my mother's killer may have stabbed to death another woman a year later but another man took the rap for it. So yes, that same killer could have remained dormant for years before returning to the parkway to go after other vulnerable women."

"Wow." Novak uttered an expletive. "Hard to believe the same killer from thirty years ago would be around to target others today and think he could get away with it."

"Why wouldn't he think that?" Garrett challenged him while wondering if Novak himself could be involved somehow with the recent killings. "After all, he got away with it before. Maybe more than once."

Novak wrinkled his nose. "If that's the case, I hope you get the bastard. But I'm afraid I still can't help you. As I said, I lost the knife, so…"

"Did you lose it, or was the knife stolen, as you claimed thirty years ago?" Madison pressed him.

"Stolen," Novak insisted. "*Lost* was just a poor choice of words."

Garrett wondered if that was the case. Or could it mean he was lying about both options and had, in fact, handed the knife off to someone?

Removing the sketch from the pocket of his khaki pants, Garrett said, "This person was seen in the vicinity of the area on the Blue Ridge Parkway where my mother was murdered. Does he look familiar?"

Novak took the sketch and studied it for a long moment before replying unevenly, "Can't say that he does…sorry."

"Take another look," Garrett insisted, sensing that he could be holding back for some reason.

Novak again stared at the drawing stoically. "Nope." He handed the sketch back to Garrett. "It's been thirty years, so my memory could be failing me. Not to mention it's just a sketch that may or may not even be an accurate portrayal of the person it's supposed to. Either way, it doesn't ring a bell. I wish I could say otherwise, but I can't."

Garrett glanced at Madison, whose expression matched his own in believing they might have reached a dead end here. If Novak did know something, he was unwilling to say so. And they were in no position to apply more pressure. "By the way," Garrett put out, "just for the record, I'll need you to account for your whereabouts when the two recent murders occurred on the parkway."

Novak gave him the dates and time frame. He claimed he'd been on his ranch those mornings in question and had ranch hands who could verify this. When they heard footsteps, Garrett turned to see Novak's daughter walking toward them in her tailored ankle booties.

"You're still here?" she questioned, eyeing them suspiciously.

"We were just leaving," Garrett told her, knowing where to find her father, should they need to interview him further. He took out his ISB business card and handed it to Novak. "If you happen to remember anything pertinent to our investigation, you can reach me on my cell phone."

Novak nodded. "I'll keep that in mind."

"Thanks for your time," Madison told him in a sociable tone of voice. She gazed at Dominique. "Have a nice day."

On that note, Garrett signaled to Madison that it

was time to go. They walked away, leaving the father and daughter standing there staring, undoubtedly.

Once out of ear range, he commented, "I'm not totally convinced that Neil Novak is as oblivious as he claims to be regarding the supposedly stolen knife. Or lack of recognition of the unsub in the sketch, for that matter."

"Neither am I," she said. "But between his insistence that the knife was stolen and his alibi then and apparent one now, we can only take a wait-and-see approach while continuing the investigation."

"Yeah, I suppose," Garrett muttered.

They walked back to his vehicle as his thoughts turned to wondering if he had missed something in the overall scheme of things in pursuing one or more killers with a common theme and deadly intentions.

HOURS LATER, Madison was still weighing whether or not Neil Novak was on the level in his assertions of playing no part in the death of Jessica Sneed or, in fact, had succeeded in pulling the wool over the eyes of investigators for decades, when she was notified over the radio that another dead woman had been found on the parkway.

Madison's heart lurched against her chest as she phoned Garrett with the distressing news. "We have a new problem," she almost hated to say, with his mother's cold case having resurfaced in the investigation.

He took a moment to digest the latest death and,

after giving him the location, Garrett said soberly, "I can get there in fifteen minutes or less."

"See you then." Madison hung up and headed to the scene she was closer to, fearful of what this meant in the bigger picture as her workplace was once again the center of unwanted attention.

She drove down the Blue Ridge Parkway to Milepost 364 and parked before heading on foot to the Craggy Gardens Trail that was lined with wild blueberries and numerous wildflowers and offered a stunning view of the Black Mountains.

Richard Edison approached her with a dour look on his face. "It's not good," the law enforcement ranger moaned as Madison caught sight of the body lying off the trail near gnarled sweet birch trees. "The victim has been identified as Heidi Ushijima, a twenty-five-year-old seasonal interpretive ranger for the National Park Service. She was discovered by a park visitor, Nadine Dobrev, who reported it." Richard's thick brows knitted. "Looks like she was stabbed to death."

"I was afraid of that," Madison muttered. She took a couple of steps forward for a closer look at the deceased park guide, whom she'd never had the pleasure of meeting when Heidi was still alive. Heidi had short brunette hair in a shag bob and was curled into a fetal position, while wearing a ranger's beige T-shirt, brown cargo pants and tennis shoes. Blood seeped through her clothing from multiple punctures to her torso and legs.

Madison looked away, believing that the Blue

Ridge Parkway Killer had likely struck again. She wondered if this brazen attack in a well-traveled but challenging area to navigate suggested that the unsub was a different, younger perp than Jessica Sneed's killer. Or could they still be one and the same?

She eyed Richard. "Any sign of the murder weapon?"

"Not yet." His lips pursed as he scanned the trail. "I'm guessing the unsub took it with him. Either to toss elsewhere like before or hold onto to use again if an opportunity arises."

"That's what bothers me," Madison said. She had little reason to believe that the unsub wouldn't continue to attack isolated females on the parkway. Not unless they were finally able to stop him cold. She looked up and saw Dawn Dominguez arrive.

"Not another one?" she asked.

"I think so," Madison had to say sadly.

Dawn frowned, making her way to the corpse. "Let's have a look."

"Someone really went to work on her," Richard said bleakly.

"Same as the others," she concurred. Wearing nitrile gloves, she gave the body an initial examination. "At the risk of sounding like a broken record, I'd say she was stabbed seven or eight times with a long-blade knife, killing her in the process."

Madison cringed as she glanced at Richard and back. "How long ago would you estimate this happened?"

Dawn felt the skin and replied, "Still relatively

warm. I say she was attacked within the past two or three hours."

This corresponded with what Madison was thinking, as it was unlikely that the victim could have been in this location all morning without being noticed. She had no reason to believe the killer had moved the body to Craggy Gardens as opposed to catching Heidi Ushijima off guard or following her in the course of her hiking there. Either way, all the signs pointed toward this being the work of the Blue Ridge Parkway Killer. But just how long had he been at this?

GARRETT ARRIVED AT the crime scene at the same time as Tom Hutchison. The strain on the face of Madison's boss was indicative of the gravity of the situation with a crazed and violent serial killer in the midst, as seemed to be the case. The fact that the same person could have been responsible for his mother's murder made it all the more unsettling for Garrett.

"Hey," he spoke lowly to Madison.

"It's him again," she stated surely.

Garrett swallowed. "Talk to me."

She brought him up to speed on the death of Heidi Ushijima in a manner that measured up to the recent murders on the parkway. It was disturbing to Garrett, to say the least, on more levels than one.

"Same old story," Madison complained. "See for yourself."

Garrett looked at the latest victim, more or less

validating his greatest fears that this case had taken another deadly turn. "Seems that way."

"What is going on?" Tom's tone was boisterous with disbelief as he homed in on the body and glared at the deputy chief medical examiner.

"We're definitely looking at a homicide due to stabbing repeatedly," she declared.

Tom pressed down on his hat. "This is starting to get out of hand," he griped.

"Not just 'starting to,'" Garrett begged to differ. "Someone has taken it upon himself to use the parkway as his personal hunting ground. We can't let him get away with it."

"Seems to me he's doing just that." Tom sighed. "Do we need more manpower to track him down?"

Without answering this, Garrett said, "What we need most is to keep from panicking and realize that, in spite of his track record, the perp is only human and, whether he knows it or not, is running out of steam."

At least I want to believe that, Garrett told himself. There were only so many ways the perp could go to commit his heinous crimes and try to hide from it in a despicable cowardly manner. Whether or not they were searching for his mother's killer, the need to restore some sense of safety on the parkway and the general area itself had never been greater.

"I agree," Richard said, furrowing his brow. "Whoever's doing this seems to be acting in desperation right now. This tells me that, apart from being a loose cannon, he's also leaving the door open for us to catch him."

"We just need to find that door, which happens to be somewhere in the vast Pisgah Ranger District," Madison pitched in, "making it that much more challenging."

"Please hurry up," Dawn said, a seriousness to her tone as she removed her gloves. "Believe it or not, I do have other dead bodies that need tending to."

"We get it," Garrett said, recognizing that they were all on the same page in the search for justice. He turned to Madison and Richard. "Find out all you can on the movements today of Heidi Ushijima, leading up to her death. Where she went. Where she lived. Why she chose to go to the Craggy Gardens. If she came here alone. You know the score."

Madison nodded. "Understood."

"Shouldn't be too difficult," Richard said. "Most of the seasonal workers hang out together and probably know one another's secrets, if there are any."

Garrett hoped that provided some answers. He said, "In the meantime, let's get the crime scene investigators out here and see what they can come up with in forensic evidence that might lead to a killer."

"On their way," Madison informed him, not too surprisingly.

"Good." They would coordinate their efforts with the local law enforcement in securing the perimeter, closing some roads leading to this part of the parkway and seeing if there were witnesses to track down and surveillance video to access. Garrett had to wonder if the unsub had left behind enough clues that hadn't been compromised by the terrain in which the corpse had been left, that could line up with other evidence gathered along the way with the clock ticking.

Chapter Sixteen

Once the body had been carted off to the morgue and the reality sank in of another murder on the Blue Ridge Parkway, Madison and Richard set out separately to see what clues they could find in the lead-up to Heidi Ushijima's death. By all accounts, the Japanese American Duke University graduate student had been well liked and had embraced her job as a seasonal interpretive ranger for the National Park Service. Madison was told by other park workers that Heidi had been in her element in teaching visitors about the parkway and Pisgah National Forest's history and cultural significance.

It was in this context of information gathering that she had apparently hiked to the Craggy Gardens, along with fellow seasonal interpretive ranger Quentin Enriques, whom Heidi had been said to be dating. But only he'd emerged alive. When Richard radioed her to say that he had located Quentin on the Cumberland Knob Trail at Milepost 217.5, Madison responded, "I'm just a few minutes away."

"He's not going anywhere," the ranger assured her.

As she drove to the location, Madison's immediate thought was could Quentin Enriques have been callous and confident enough to stab Heidi to death and then go about his business as though nothing had happened? If so, she imagined he would have needed to dispose of his bloody clothing somewhere along the way. Along with the murder weapon. Was this feasible? Or had Heidi encountered someone else at Craggy Gardens?

I have to keep all options on the table, Madison reminded herself. Just as Garrett was doing, in spite of his being drawn to the specter of his mother's murder in relation to the current happenings.

Madison reached the Cumberland Knob in Alleghany County, near the North Carolina-Virginia border, and parked. The site, which combined woodlands with open spaces, was popular for viewing different birds and wildlife. She spotted Richard talking with a tall and stocky twentysomething male with brown hair in a half-bun ponytail. He had separated the suspect from a group of tourists.

"This is Ranger Lynley," Richard told him and said to her, "I've just informed Quentin about the murder of Heidi Ushijima. He claims she was alive and well when they split up."

"This is crazy." Quentin's lower lip quivered. "Heidi's dead?"

Madison saw the distress in his face and brown eyes that seemed genuine enough. She still had to ask, "When did you last see Heidi?"

"About three hours ago, when we were together at Craggy Gardens."

"Why did you leave?"

"I needed to move on to my next assignment," he pointed out, "exploring the Cumberland Knob area with visitors."

Sounds plausible, Madison thought. She glanced at the tourists, who were taking pictures of the surroundings and seemed only mildly curious. "Did you see anyone else on the Craggy Gardens Trail?"

Quentin shrugged. "I passed by some people here or there, but no one who was traveling alone," he claimed. "Or otherwise seemed suspicious at the time."

Richard peered at him. "I understand that you and Heidi were dating?"

"Yeah, we hung out," Quentin admitted. "It wasn't anything serious. We were both just here for the summer."

"So, you didn't have a fight or anything at Craggy Gardens?" Richard questioned.

"No," he insisted. "We were cool."

"Did Heidi ever indicate to you that she wasn't cool with someone else?" Madison posed to him. "Either within the NPS or outside of it?"

Quentin shook his head. "If she was having a problem with anyone, Heidi never shared it with me."

Madison gazed at him while thinking that, given his age, at the very least he didn't square with a person old enough to have murdered Jessica Sneed. But might there have been some other connection between the killer then and now?

"Sorry we had to put you through this," she voiced sympathetically, giving him the benefit of the doubt that he was another innocent secondary victim of murder.

"You're just doing your job," he muttered.

"We may need to talk to you again," Richard cautioned him. "But for now, you're free to rejoin your group, if you like."

"Or take some time off to grieve," Madison told Quentin.

They had no reason to hold him further, she realized. It wouldn't make dealing with Heidi's death any easier for him or them. When Quentin walked away with his head down, Madison surmised, "He didn't kill her. No signs of being cut himself. Or being able to dispose of the evidence and return to his duties without missing a beat."

"I was thinking the same thing," Richard said, frowning. "We'll keep at it."

Madison nodded. Once back in her car, she phoned Garrett with an update. "So far, we've hit a brick wall among Heidi's colleagues and the guy she was dating. He's only in his twenties, by the way," she threw out, conflicting with the cold to new cases homicide theory.

"Heidi was likely killed by someone outside her workplace or social circles," Garrett argued. "As to the age disparity in connecting the serial killer to my mother's murder, there's always the possibility of a copycat killer."

She agreed. "There is that."

"If this proves to be true or the Blue Ridge Parkway Killer of today is unconnected to a thirty-year-old homicide that stays a cold case, I'll have to accept that."

So would she. But for now, Madison still trusted his instincts and had to believe the link was there in some way, shape or fashion. "As long as the co-investigations persist, we'll just have to see where they take us."

"All right."

When they disconnected, Madison found herself looking ahead and knowing that they made a great team. Love did that to people who connected on a deep level. It was something that she hoped would blossom into an even greater appreciation of one another.

"IN LIGHT OF the latest homicide on the Blue Ridge Parkway, I've gotten the go-ahead from my boss, Wilma Seatriz, in Washington, DC, to raise the reward to fifty thousand dollars for any meaningful information that leads to the arrest and prosecution of the unsub," Carly told Garrett an hour after he had updated her on the murder of Heidi Ushijima.

He was at his temporary cabin, video chatting on his laptop with the South Atlantic-Gulf regional director. Carly had managed to convince Seatriz, the NPS associate director for visitor and resource protection, who oversaw the Division of Law Enforcement, Security, and Emergency Services that Garrett worked for, of the importance in upping the ante to catch a killer. Though Garrett hated the thought of paying money for a solid lead, he hated even more the reality that the unsub had managed to elude them thus far. As such, with three women recently stabbed to death on the parkway and at least one murdered decades ago by perhaps the same killer, it was imperative that they use every means at their disposal to get justice. Whether or not doubling the reward would do the trick was anyone's guess.

I'm definitely on board with giving this a shot, Garrett told himself. "That's good," he said. "The public can still play an important role in solving this case."

"Maybe it won't need to come to that," Carly argued, wrinkling her nose. "I mean, we have the finest federal investigators in the business, starting with yourself. If anyone can crack this case the good old-fashioned way, it's you, Sneed."

Garrett resisted a grin, flattered by the suggestion while feeling the pressure of being put on a sneaky pedestal. He also read between the lines. She would rather they keep the cash in the federal coffers, if at all possible, to have handy for another day. "I'll see what I can do" was the best he could promise, while knowing she fully expected that and then some.

Carly waited a beat, then asked, "Are you still angling the parkway serial killer as being connected with the death of your mother?"

Garrett sat back, thoughtful. "I have no proof of that," he admitted, "but looking at it squarely, I believe it to be a real possibility that the unsub has crossed decades in taking lives and has either simply gotten lucky or maybe was incarcerated for committing other crimes, only to resume targeting women in the Blue Ridge Mountains once freed."

"Well, I trust your instincts," she said assuredly. "On that note, I've asked a criminologist that the NPS has worked with in the past to speak with you about the investigation."

"Oh…?"

"Her name is Katrina Sherwood. She specializes in serial killer cases, has written three books and may be able to give you some added perspective in trying to track down the Blue Ridge Parkway Killer."

As if he could refuse what amounted to a directive from his superior, not that he would turn down assistance from an expert on serial killers, Garrett responded, "I'd be happy to speak with Ms. Sherwood."

Carly smiled. "I'll text you her number, and you can give her a call."

"I'll do that," he promised.

"Keep me posted on the investigation."

Garrett nodded. "I will."

After ending the conversation, he left his makeshift office and grabbed a beer from the refrigerator. He thought about Madison and how much they had managed to recapture since starting over. He relished being able to take this and run with it, no matter the distance, in wanting to find that dream of a life together at the end of the rainbow.

Walking back into the living room, Garrett lifted

up his cell phone and saw the number Carly had texted for Katrina Sherwood.

No time like the present, he thought, in giving her a call.

She answered after two rings with, "Katrina."

"Hi. I'm Special Agent Garrett Sneed," he told her. "Carly Tafoya asked me to contact you regarding a case I'm working on."

"Right. The Blue Ridge Parkway murder investigation," she acknowledged. "Carly brought me up to speed on where things stand and the possible cold-case connection."

"Okay." Garrett felt this was a step in right direction.

"Why don't we switch to video," Katrina requested. "It's better for a real dialogue. Don't you think?"

"Absolutely." He sat down on a wingback accent chair and tapped the Video icon on the phone. Katrina Sherwood appeared. African American and attractive, she was in her forties with bold brown eyes and curly blond hair in a Deva cut.

She flashed her teeth. "Nice to meet you, Agent Sneed."

"You too," he said evenly.

"Why don't we get down to business," she told him. "You're dealing with a serial killer in your midst who's stabbing to death women on the parkway, right?"

"Yes. He's apparently picking his victims at random but may also have been stalking them before things took a deadly turn."

"Typical," Katrina asserted matter-of-factly. "That is to say, it's typical that many serial killers seek out victims randomly, but just as many others may have stalked their victims for a while and then killed them when the best opportunity presented itself to do so. There are no absolutes when it comes to serial homicide and the heterogeneous nature and characteristics of the offenders," she stressed, "apart from the fact that a serial killer by definition kills two or more people in separate incidents, which I'm sure you understand."

"I do," Garrett conceded, "all too well. I am curious, though, as to your take on why stab the victims instead of, say, shooting or strangling them, given the messiness of a stabbing attack."

"Frankly, most stabbing serial killers give little thought to the messy nature of such assaults. Think Jack the Ripper, John Eichinger or Kenneth Granviel, to name a few." She twisted her lips musingly. "Some serial killers simply choose stabbing over other ways to kill because they get some kind of perverse thrill in the violence and suffering that goes along with it. Other serial killers may choose a knife as a more accessible weapon or easier to use to kill than say, trying to strangle the victim. Yet other serial killers may view inflicting pain upon another as a power grab."

Garrett grimaced as he pictured his mother being victimized this way. Though he had some idea, he asked, "Why start killing, only to stop for years or even decades before starting back up again?"

Katrina narrowed her eyes. "You're thinking about the murder of your mother, thirty years ago?"

"Yeah," Garrett confirmed and took a sip of his beer. "And the possibility that her killer may have killed another woman a year later, then laid low for decades, only to rediscover stabbing to death vulnerable females."

"I see." She took a breath. "Well, killers stop killing for all types of reasons," she explained. "These include fear of being caught, illness, romance, imprisonment for another crime or just deciding enough was enough. In the case of The Ripper, for example, the unsub apparently ended his killing ways abruptly after 1888, by some accounts, and never resuming. On the other hand, Lonnie David Franklin Jr., a serial killer also known as the Grim Sleeper, took a fourteen-year hiatus between killings. Similarly, serial killer Dennis Rader, aka the BTK Strangler, went over a decade since his last kill before being captured.

"My point is that if the man who killed your mother has resurfaced after all these years to target other women, assuming he hadn't kept it going elsewhere in the country, it could be for any number of reasons. These include boredom, death in the family, an impulsive desire to get back in the game, opportunistic circumstances or an aura of invincibility, having been successful the first time around without getting caught."

Garrett gave an understanding nod. "I get where you're coming from," he told her bleakly. It also gave him food for uneasy thoughts to gnaw on. Had his mother's killer come back to terrorize the Blue Ridge Mountains and Pisgah Ranger District once again? Or had another staked his claim in following suit as the Blue Ridge Parkway Killer?

THE KILLER HIKED in the mountainous forest and meadows. He enjoyed the solitude on the Blue Ridge Parkway, though at times encountering elk, peregrine falcons, white-tailed deer, wild turkeys and even a black bear every now and then. It was nature at its finest, and he was part of it. The fact that he had killed more than once and planned to do so again was who he was at his core. As was the case for any animal predator he ran into.

He continued to make his way through hollows and coves, mountain ash and yellow birch trees, and black huckleberry shrubs en route to his destination. Whistling, he broke the silence, save for the sporadic sounds of indigo buntings and red-winged blackbirds meandering through the trees. His thoughts moved to Heidi Ushijima, his latest victim. A flicker of guilt ripped through him that he'd taken her life. It disappeared in an instant, realizing that it was something that'd had to be done.

He had known beforehand that Heidi had had to die. The only question had been when. She'd provided him the answer when he'd overheard her talking about heading to the Craggy Gardens Trail. Accompanying her had been another seasonal interpretive ranger, Quentin Enriques. He had watched the two kissing from time to time, making it clear that they'd been sweet on one another.

Given that the desire to kill Heidi had nearly overcome all reason, he might have had to take out Quentin too. Only after a while, he'd left Craggy Gardens alone to go elsewhere. Then some others had come along, and Heidi exchanged pleasantries with them before they, too, had moved on. That was when it had been time to make his move. While Heidi had been preoccupied with wildflowers, he'd taken her totally by surprise. At first, recognizing him, she'd actually believed he'd simply been out and about.

Only when she'd seen the new eight-inch serrated knife he'd produced, after ditching the last one, had the small talk come to a screeching halt. When she'd tried to make a run for it, he'd anticipated her move and surprised her by being quicker. He'd caught up to her and gone to work with the knife. Ignoring her cries, he'd finished the job in short order. He'd thought he'd heard someone coming and made his planned escape, using his knowledge of the parkway to hide from sight. When the coast had been clear, he'd continued to put distance between himself and his latest victim.

He reached his tent and felt as though it offered him the sanctuary he needed—till it was time to move on to greener pastures, where he could start fresh in appeasing his deadly appetite. But not before he could turn his attention to the pretty law enforcement ranger, Madison Lynley, who in time would soon come to feel her life being drained away when he struck time and time again with his blade.

Chapter Seventeen

"Agent Sneed," the raspy voice said. "This is Neil Novak."

Garrett was driving that morning when the call came. "How can I help you, Mr. Novak?" he asked coolly, though more than curious in hearing from the rancher.

"We need to talk," Novak said tersely.

So talk, Garrett thought, wondering if this would be a confession. "I'm listening."

"In person," he insisted.

"All right," Garrett told him. "I can be at your ranch in twenty minutes."

"Actually, I'd like to speak at my attorney's office."

With that, Garrett assumed what he had to say might constitute legal jeopardy and piqued his own interest all the more. "Not a problem."

"Her name's Pauline Vasquez," Novak said. "She's with the Eugenio, Debicki and Vasquez law firm in the Kiki Place Office Building on Twelfth Street and Bentmoore."

"I know where it is," Garrett said. He remembered

Madison interviewing Pauline Vasquez about murder victim Olivia Forlani when they visited the law firm a few days ago. Was Vasquez's representation of Novak coincidental? Or something more unsettling in the scheme of things? "I'll be there," Garrett told him, agreeing to meet in half an hour.

"By the way," Novak said, a catch to his voice, "bring that sketch with you."

"Uh, okay." Garrett tried to read into that. Was he actually ready to come clean about the unsub in the composite drawing?

After disconnecting, Garrett glanced at the cowhide leather messenger bag on the passenger seat. It contained the sketch of the unsub and other case materials.

He phoned Madison on the parkway and said, "You won't believe who I just got a call from."

"Who?" she asked.

"Neil Novak."

"Really?"

"He has something to say," Garrett told her. "But will only do so in the presence of his lawyer, who happens to be Pauline Vasquez."

"No kidding?"

"I kid you not." He paused. "Novak has asked to take another look at the sketch of the unsub."

"Interesting," Madison hummed. "When is this meeting taking place?"

He told her and said keenly, "You should be there."

"Wouldn't miss it," she assured him. "If Neil Novak has something to get off his chest with legal representation, it must be something huge."

"Yeah, that's what I was thinking." Garrett gazed at the road ahead. "Let me know where you are, and we can drive there together." She gave him her location, and he went for her, knowing that Madison's curiosity was piqued as much as his in what this was all about. He longed for the day when they could spend even more time together on their own terms.

MADISON SAT IN an accent chair beside Garrett on one side of a white rectangular meeting table in a conference room with a wide floor-to-ceiling window. On the other side was Neil Novak; his daughter, Dominique Novak; and their attorney, Pauline Vasquez. One could hear a pin drop, making Madison wonder just where this was going in relation to their criminal investigation.

After a tense moment or two, Pauline pasted a thin smile on her lips and said, "Thanks for coming, Special Agent Sneed and Ranger Lynley."

Garrett leaned forward. "So, exactly why are we here?" he cut to the chase. For her part, Madison couldn't help but think that it could have been her friend Olivia representing the firm in this matter, had the partnership not been handed to Pauline prior to Olivia's death, without her ever being the wiser.

"My client, Mr. Novak, has information he believes to be relevant to your investigation into a cold case," the attorney responded. "But to be clear, the info is strictly voluntarily given and implies no guilt or knowledge beforehand."

"Got it," Garrett told her laconically and gazed at Novak. "What would you like to say to us?"

Novak scratched his beard. "Did you bring the sketch?"

"Yeah." Garrett produced it and slid it across the table.

Novak picked it up and studied it for a beat before setting the sketch back down. He sucked in a deep breath and uttered, "I've seen him before."

"Where?" Madison asked. "When?"

"Asheville," he asserted. "Thirty years ago."

"Did you know him?" Garrett asked straightforwardly.

"Yeah, I knew who he was, but we weren't friends or anything."

"Do you recall his name?" Madison asked, peering at him.

"Deschanel, I believe…" Novak said after a moment or two. "Yeah, it was Bryan Deschanel."

Taking his word on this for now, Madison watched Garrett make a note to that effect; then he asked him bluntly, "Did you give Bryan Deschanel the knife that was used to kill Jessica Sneed?"

"No, definitely not!" Novak insisted. "I can't even say if he was the one who took my knife. I do remember seeing him hanging around my truck but never made the connection between that and the stolen knife." He drew a breath. "Not till you showed me the sketch yesterday."

Garrett frowned. "So, you lied to a federal law enforcement officer when questioned about the sketch? Not a smart move."

"I didn't want to get involved," he claimed. "Apart from that, I couldn't be sure at the time without seeing the sketch again that it was the same guy I thought it might be."

"Are you saying you never saw the sketch before we showed it to you?" Madison asked, knowing that it had been part of the official investigation back in the day. How could he, as a person of interest and suspect, not have been shown the sketch?

"Never!" Novak asserted. "Don't ask me why, but the police never showed up at my door with this and I never saw it in the newspaper. Otherwise, I would've said something."

"My dad's telling you the truth," Dominique spoke up, tucking hair behind her ear. "It was me who talked him into coming forward and saying what he knew. Or thought he did. He would never have tried to impede a murder investigation. Or cover up for a killer."

"That should be obvious, just by us being here right now," Pauline argued. "My client is doing his civic duty by telling you what he knows. What you do with it is up to you, but as Mr. Novak was cleared of any involvement three decades ago, this is where his obligation as a citizen ends."

Garrett relaxed his rigid jawline. "We have no desire to go after your client, Ms. Vasquez," he told her.

She smiled. "Good."

"But we do have a few more questions for him," Garrett said.

Novak met his gaze. "Go ahead."

"Have you seen Bryan Deschanel lately?"

"Haven't seen him in thirty years," Novak alleged. "If I saw him on the street, I doubt I'd even recognize him today. Beyond that, as I recall him being a trouble-maker who others thought was messed up in the head, he's not someone I'd want in my life or my daughter's."

"What kind of trouble?" Garrett asked him.

"He had anger issues and was prone to violence and vandalism."

Madison couldn't help but think about the vicious-ness of the attack on Jessica Sneed as well as the three recent victims of fatal stabbings. Could Bryan Deschanel have been responsible for all of these?

She eyed Novak and said, "It's possible that Des-chanel is still around and is now targeting women on the Blue Ridge Parkway. Including a third woman stabbed to death since we last spoke to you."

"Yeah, heard about that." Novak lowered his chin. "Made me wonder if there could be a connection of some sort with what happened thirty years ago."

"I wondered too," Dominique said. "When my father told me about the possibility that the same person who murdered your mother, Agent Sneed, could be doing it again, I managed to convince him that he needed to do the right thing and speak up. And we are."

Garrett nodded. "I appreciate your coming for-ward," he told them.

"If it can help you solve your case, it will have been well worth my trouble," Novak said.

Pauline rested her arm on her leather briefcase and said, "I understand that there's a fifty-thousand-dollar reward on the table for information leading to the arrest and conviction of the so-called Blue Ridge Parkway Killer?"

Madison frowned. "So, this is all about money?" *Blood money*, she thought.

"It's not what you think," she responded quickly and turned to the Novaks.

Dominique sat up straight. "We don't care about the money," she stressed. "But if for whatever reason we qualify for receiving it, we intend to donate every cent to organizations that focus on violence against women." She sucked in a deep breath. "Five years ago, I lost my mother to such a senseless act."

As Dominique's words sank in, Madison stood corrected on her initial assumptions and said sincerely, "I'm sorry to hear about your mother."

She nodded, and Novak said, "So, as you see, Agent Sneed, we have more in common than you thought."

"Guess we do," Garrett conceded.

"Anyway, any such reward would all be facilitated through Ms. Vasquez," Dominique stated.

"We would certainly see to it that their wishes were carried out to the letter," Pauline assured them.

Garrett responded, "Whether or not the information given to us results in anything is still up in the air. Right now, our goal in representing the National Park Service is to try to locate Bryan Deschanel and see what he's been up to. Or may have been running from for the past three decades."

Pauline smoothed a brow. "I understand."

"We'll be in touch," Madison said as the meeting adjourned and she left with Garrett, equipped with intel on a person of interest in both a cold case and one that seemed to be getting hotter with each passing day.

"You think Bryan Deschanel is alive and well, lurking around the Blue Ridge Parkway, killing women?" Madison asked point-blank as Garrett drove down Hayten Road.

It was a good question, he knew, and one they both needed an answer to, one way or the other. "My gut tells me that Deschanel is still among the living," Garrett said flatly. "And that he may be closer than we think."

"And your mother's killer?"

"Yes." There was no sugarcoating this. Garrett cringed at the thought. "When you put the pieces together, beginning with the unsub's sketch ID'd by Neil Novak—I think that Deschanel stole the knife from Novak's pickup, used it on my mother and likely attacked another woman the following year. I believe he's been lying low ever since. At least till recently, when deciding to resurface on the parkway and use his guiles to murder more women, while operating with impunity in plain sight. I'm betting that the latent palm print Jewel pulled from the survival knife used to kill Olivia Forlani and Nicole Wallenberg belongs to Deschanel and no other."

"I think you may be spot on," Madison stated. "We need to find Deschanel, wherever he's hiding, and hold him accountable for his crimes."

"Right." Garrett turned onto Overlook Road and approached the Blue Ridge Parkway. "I'll run a criminal background check on Bryan Deschanel and see what else I can learn about the man and his whereabouts. In the meantime, be extra careful on the parkway while he's still on the loose and dangerous as ever."

"I will," she promised, placing a hand on his shoulder. "You too. I have a feeling that Deschanel, evidently used to having his way, is a threat to anyone who comes into contact with him."

"I agree." Garrett grinned at her. "I can take whatever he dishes out and give back thrice as hard."

Madison smiled warmly. "I'm sure you can."

He knew she was capable of handling herself too and was armed, while having backup among other rangers. But till they had the dangerous suspect in custody, Garrett doubted he'd be able to relax and feel confident that she was out of harm's way. That was something he couldn't afford to take for granted.

Chapter Eighteen

Garrett went back to his cabin and, on the laptop, dug into Bryan Deschanel's criminal background and any other information that was accessible. Running his name through local law enforcement databases, the National Crime Information Center, the North Carolina DMV, the FBI's Next Generation Identification system, and various social media sites, Garrett found that Deschanel had no criminal record, per se, or outstanding warrants. Nor did his name show up in a Google search, on Facebook, Instagram or Twitter.

But Bryan Deschanel had been a person of interest in the death of his mother, Garrett noted, when digging deeper into police reports, and newspaper accounts in a search on Google. Helena Deschanel had died in a mysterious house fire when Deschanel had been in his late teens. Though suspected of causing the fire, police had lacked the evidence to prove it, and he'd been let off the hook. In his twenties, Deschanel had had other skirmishes with the law but had never been charged with a crime. He'd once been accused of domestic violence, but the victim had inexplicably withdrawn her complaint.

Garrett cocked a brow when he discovered that Bryan Deschanel had been an early suspect in the stabbing death of twenty-nine-year-old Vicki Flanagan, who'd been killed on the Blue Ridge Parkway by the Yadkin Valley Overlook a year after the murder of Garrett's mother. Blake O'Donnell, who'd confessed to the crime and then recanted, had been ultimately convicted for it. *What if Deschanel was the true culprit and O'Donnell innocent after all?* Garrett wondered.

He went through the files again that ex-Sheriff Lou Buckley had lent them in the investigation, looking for any mention of Bryan Deschanel. Garrett found it. Deschanel had been questioned briefly as a potential witness by a deputy, but somehow no connection had been made between him and the sketch of the unsub. It made Garrett wonder if he was off base in suspecting Bryan Deschanel of being a three-decades-long serial killer.

Not when I look at this squarely, he told himself. The circumstantial evidence was there. Some physical evidence too, that might link the suspect to at least two of the murders. Along with too many facts that, when put together, had to be more than merely coincidental. Still, Garrett was troubled that Deschanel was not showing up on the radar. And hadn't apparently in years. Could he be dead, with someone else stepping into his shoes as a serial killer?

Garrett went even further in searching for evidence that Bryan Deschanel was no longer alive. Nothing came up in a Google search or other data. It was almost as though the man had dropped off the face of the earth. *I'm not buying it*, Garrett thought. He cross-checked Deschanel's name for any possible aliases that might be known to authorities. Nothing registered, frustrating him.

Still, the idea that Bryan Deschanel had either engaged in identity theft or simply created from scratch or know-how a moniker he was going by to more easily operate without his past catching up to him was gaining steam with Garrett. He was all but certain that the murder suspect was not only alive and well but living or working within the vicinity of the Blue Ridge Parkway.

Garrett grabbed the sketch and studied it. But that was from thirty years ago. If Deschanel was still alive, what did he look like today? With that thought in mind and no known actual photograph of the suspect, Garrett believed that an age-progression sketch of Deschanel would give him a more accurate image to work with and circulate to other law enforcement.

He got on his cell phone and requested a video chat with Caitlin Rundle, a forensic artist at the North Carolina State Bureau of Investigation that the National Park Service had used in other criminal investigations. Thirtysomething, she was following in the footsteps of her father, Karl Rundle, a retired renowned crime-scene sketch artist. Caitlin accepted the call after three rings.

"Agent Sneed," she said, gazing back at him through blue eyes, with short blond hair framing her face.

"Hey, Caitlin." Garrett straightened his shoulders. "I need a big favor."

"Sure. How can I help?"

"I'm investigating a thirty-year-old cold-case homicide," he explained. "All I have right now on my chief suspect is a hand-drawn sketch that was done of him at the time. I need a better representation of what he might look like today."

Caitlin smiled. "I think I can assist you with that," she said with confidence. "Just send me what you have, and I'll do my best to give you a digitally enhanced image that is age appropriate for the unsub today."

"Wonderful." Garrett's eyes crinkled at the corners. "How soon do you need it?"

"Would yesterday be soon enough?" he responded dryly.

She gave a little chuckle. "I'll get on it right away."

"Great." He gave her the relevant information he had on the serial killer suspect, including a digital picture of the composite drawing of him.

While Garrett waited to hear back from Caitlin, he again studied the clues that led him to believe that Bryan Deschanel was still alive, responsible for at least four murders by stabbing and posed a serious threat to even more women on the Blue Ridge Parkway.

MADISON WAS SITTING in her car, reading the chilling autopsy report on the latest female to die on the parkway. According to the deputy chief medical examiner,

Heidi had been the victim of numerous stabbings—
had been attacked with a knife seven times—to her
back, buttocks and legs, resulting in death by homicide. The murder weapon was described as a sharp
serrated-edge knife with an eight-inch blade.

What a monster, Madison told herself, hating that
another fellow ranger had been brutally murdered in
an unprovoked, callous assault. The fact that such
a picturesque and usually hospitable setting as the
Blue Ridge Mountains and Pisgah National Forest
had been turned into a killing field made it all the
harder to digest. Worse was that there was a good
chance the perpetrator had also murdered Garrett's
mother and managed to get away with it.

Till now. With Bryan Deschanel being fingered
as the man in the thirty-year-old sketch, at the very
least, this told them that he was likely Jessica's killer.
And had quite possibly murdered another woman the
following year. Though much older now, the stars
lined up to the notion that he might have come back
to carry on his homicidal tendencies today. If so, now
that they had drawn a bead on him, it was just a matter of time before his reign of terror was over. Until
then, Madison hoped that no other woman would see
her life cut short by a madman.

When she got a call over the radio, Madison heard
Leonard say with a sense of urgency, "We just got a
report of a woman injured below the Raven Rocks
Overlook."

The spot immediately struck a chord with Madison. It was the very area where Jessica Sneed had

been killed. Had her killer done a repeat performance thirty years later?

"I'm on my way," Madison told Leonard.

Afterward, she relayed this to Richard and Tom, calling for backup while hoping they could quickly seal off any escape routes.

Madison drove to the parking area for the Raven Rocks Overlook. She spotted a gray metallic Land Rover parked there. Getting out of her car, Madison approached the vehicle cautiously. It was unoccupied but had tourist brochures spread out on the front passenger seat. Did this car belong to the injured woman?

Peeking below the overlook, Madison saw nothing unusual. She wondered if this could be someone's idea of a practical joke. It had been known to happen sometimes on the parkway. Usually the work of mischievous teenagers. But given the recent happenings on the parkway, Madison had to believe that a woman might truly be in distress and needed her help.

She made her way down the incline and headed toward the woods, where she thought she heard a sound. Was it an animal? Or human? Removing her pistol from the duty holster, Madison saw Ward Wilcox, the maintenance ranger, approaching her.

"Stop," she ordered instinctively, knowing this was outside his normal work area.

He obeyed, standing rigidly. "Ranger Lynley."

"What are you doing here, Ward?" Madison eyed him suspiciously aiming the pistol at him.

"I was told I was needed," he said simply. "What

are you doing here? And why are you pointing your gun at me?"

"We received a report of an injured woman below the Raven Rocks Overlook," she told him. "Then I run into you… In light of the recent murders on the parkway, maybe I have good reason for holding you at gunpoint." Peering at the maintenance ranger, Madison wondered if she was looking at the Blue Ridge Parkway Killer. And Jessica Sneed's killer?

"Hey, I'm just as confused as you are," Ward insisted. "And I swear to you, I didn't hurt anyone. I certainly had nothing to do with the parkway deaths of those women." He took a step toward her.

"Don't come any closer!" Madison aimed the gun at Ward's chest as he stopped. "Put your hands up where I can see them, Ward. I mean it."

He complied, while saying tonelessly, "You're making a mistake. I'm innocent."

"We'll see about that." She took a couple of steps backward to put a little more distance between them and, while keeping the gun on him with one hand, removed her radio with the other to report the mysterious situation and that she was holding Ward Wilcox as a possible suspect in one or more crimes. She knew that erring on the side of caution was her smartest bet. No sooner had she gotten off the radio with help on the way that Madison heard what sounded like heavy shoes hitting the dirt behind her.

Before she could turn, Ward shrieked, "What the hell do you think you're doing?"

Suddenly, Madison felt a fist slam into the side

of her head. Blurry-eyed, she caught sight of a familiar man and thought he said something wicked to her before she went down like a rock and everything went dark.

WHEN GARRETT HEARD back from Caitlin, she said coolly, "Agent Sneed, I've finished an age-progression digital sketch of Bryan Deschanel and what he might look like today, taking into consideration some standard characteristics that typically accompany aging into one's fifties and sixties."

"Let's see what you've got," Garrett responded eagerly on the speakerphone while in his car and heading toward the Blue Ridge Parkway, where he had been trying to reach Madison, to no avail.

"I'm sending it to your cell phone right now," Caitlin told him. "Keep in mind that I did this on short notice and not from an old actual photograph. But it should give you some perspective on your person of interest."

Garrett pulled over, grabbed the phone and gazed at the age-progression composite drawing of Bryan Deschanel, causing his heart to skip a beat in shock. It was a dead ringer for someone he had met before. Ronnie Mantegna, an NPS maintenance worker. And someone who had easy access in and out of the Blue Ridge Parkway without drawing undue suspicion, while being familiar with the landscape accordingly.

"What do you think?" Caitlin asked anxiously.

"I think you did a great job," Garrett told her. "Thanks for the quick work."

"Anytime." She paused. "If you need me to further enhance the sketch for greater clarity, let me know."

"I will." He disconnected and tried to contact Madison again. Still no pickup, concerning him. Getting back on the road, he called her boss, Tom. When he answered, Garrett said, "I can't seem to reach Madison."

"She went out on a call after a woman was reported injured," he said.

"What woman?"

"We're still trying to sort it out."

Garrett tensed. "What can you tell me about Maintenance Ranger Ronnie Mantegna?"

"He's been working for us for the last six months," Tom replied. "Let me take a quick look at his file... He's fifty-six, never married, has wilderness experience and been good at his job. Why do you ask?"

"I think that Ronnie Mantegna is an alias for Bryan Deschanel," Garrett said without prelude. "The man I believe to be responsible for my mother's murder thirty years ago and the Blue Ridge Parkway killings today."

Tom grunted and said, "Tell me more..."

Garrett gave a rundown of his solid case against Mantegna and sent Tom the age-progression digital image. "He's been right before our eyes the entire time I've been back here," Garrett stated knowingly. "And may be the one targeting another woman on the parkway now."

Tom mouthed an expletive. "We need to warn Ranger Lynley." He sighed exasperatedly. "Except I haven't been able to reach her either."

"Where did she go to respond to the injured female?"

"Raven Rocks Overlook." Tom made a sound, as if to himself. "According to the GPS tracker on her vehicle, that's where Madison still is, at Milepost 289.5."

"I'm almost there," Garrett told him, ending the conversation as he put on some speed, hoping to reach the destination in time.

Bryan Deschanel must have lured Madison to Raven Rocks Overlook, he figured, where Deschanel had stabbed to death his mother so long ago. Now in some sort of warped homicidal impulse, under the cover of his moniker Ronnie Mantegna or not, Deschanel planned to let history repeat itself by taking Madison's life in the same manner, Garrett couldn't help but sense.

I have to stop that bastard from killing the true love of my life—destroying any chance at a long-term future together. The thought that Mantegna could succeed in taking away another person so near and dear to him, decades apart, was unbearable to Garrett. He reached Milepost 289.5 and raced to the Raven Rocks Overlook.

MADISON OPENED HER eyes to a splitting headache, feeling as though she had been someone's punching bag. It took a long moment of trying to regain her equilibrium before she remembered what had happened. She'd been facing Ward Wilcox, believing he might have harmed a woman near the Raven Rocks Overlook and done even worse things, when someone had clocked Madison from behind. Her first thought was that maybe Ward had been partnered in crime with another person. But then she recalled right before being sucker punched that Ward had seemed just as unprepared for the moment and to be trying to warn her of impending danger. Before it had been too late.

"I see you're awake," she heard the familiar voice.

Realizing she was on the ground in a wooded area, Madison ignored the pounding in her head and turned her face slightly to the right. Hovering above her was Ronnie Mantegna, a maintenance ranger.

"Ronnie…" she managed as the wheels began to churn in the perilous moment she faced. Especially while taking note of the long-bladed serrated knife he was holding.

"Actually, my real name's Bryan Deschanel," he said smugly. "I'm guessing you've already come to the realization that I'm the one who knocked you out."

Madison knew she needed to play dumb while trying to figure out how she could still get out of this alive. "Why did you hit me?" she asked innocently. "And where's Ward?"

"You're entitled to know those answers. First question. I hit you because I needed to relieve you of your firearm without the risk of getting shot in the process. Plus, it was easier for my other plans for you." Deschanel glanced at the gun stuck inside his pants at the waist. "I'm the one you and Special Agent Sneed have been looking for."

"The Blue Ridge Parkway Killer?" Her mouth

hung open as though in total shock. In reality, the pieces of the puzzle had already begun to fall into place the moment she'd gotten a grip on the circumstances she'd found herself in.

"You got it!" His eyes lit with triumph. "I killed them, and you're next, Ranger Lynley. For the record, though, I've been at this for a long time. My first kill was my own mother. She pissed me off one too many times, and I'd had enough. Made it so the fire seemed like an accident due to faulty electrical wiring, which I knew a thing or two about. Got what she deserved." He laughed, thoughtful. "Next was Agent Sneed's mother, believe it or not, who was hiking in this very spot before we ran into each other, catching her completely by surprise, and I did what I needed to do."

Madison's head had cleared enough that she was able to sit up without feeling dizzy. But he was still brandishing the knife and had her gun. Again, she sought to be genuinely taken aback by his revelation. "You really killed Jessica Sneed?"

"Is it that hard to believe?" He laughed. "I'm only halfway into my fifties. Meaning I was just in my midtwenties back then. Same was true the following year, when I stabbed to death another unsuspecting woman on the parkway. Got away with it too, thanks partly to some other idiot volunteering to take the fall before he tried to backpedal. But it was too late."

So, he admits to killing his mother, Jessica and a third female from three decades ago and earlier, Madison told herself. *But why the long pause be-*

tween then and now? "If you got away with it, why would you risk everything by starting to kill women again?"

"Yeah, about that… It's something inside me that I can't seem to control," he argued, rubbing his jawline. "Well, in trying to fit in as a law-abiding citizen, guess I was able to control my dark impulses for a while through drugs, therapy and whatnot." Deschanel pursed his lips. "But I grew tired of playing Mr. Nice Guy and ditched the drugs and therapy. I was happy to be myself again."

So that explains the long gap between serial killings, Madison thought. Too bad his inner demons had taken over again. It did little, though, to get her out of a predicament that placed her entire future in jeopardy. One she hoped to have with Garrett. Or had that page been turned forever?

"Anyway, I lured you here by falsely reporting that a woman was in distress," the killer explained calmly. "I was counting on them sending you in particular, as this is your neck of the woods, so to speak, to patrol."

Madison sought to buy more time as she studied the woods for escape routes. "Just let me go, Ronnie or Bryan," she said. "I'll give you a head start, and you can go anywhere you'd like."

"Yeah, right." His head snapped back as he chortled. "Since you've been cozying up with Agent Sneed, something tells me you wouldn't hesitate to blab to him about what I did to his mother the moment I allowed you to live. Sorry, no can do."

"You never said what happened to Ward Wilcox," Madison questioned. She scanned the area for any signs of him but saw none. "Did you kill him too?"

"Actually, Ranger Lynley, you did," Deschanel responded with a wry chuckle. He glanced at her pistol. "After roping him into showing up here to remove debris, I forced Ward to run into the woods, then fatally shot him with your gun. That was what you managed to do just before he cut you up with his knife that I intend to place in his hands once I'm through stabbing you to death. Then I'm outta here to look for a new place to settle down and cause trouble, while getting away scot-free with the parkway murders—again."

Madison scrambled to her feet, realizing that the serial slayer had her at a disadvantage. She considered going for the gun. Perhaps the element of surprise would cause him to let down his guard long enough to take it and shoot him before he could react. But with him holding the sharp knife firmly and having shown prowess as an attacker, she wasn't comfortable with those odds.

Deschanel bristled while moving toward her. "Sorry it's come to this, but it is what it is."

Or not, Madison thought. Her first instinct was to run. Though he was obviously in good enough shape to kill and evade detection and capture, she was sure she could outrun him as a jogger. But what if she were wrong? What if he proved to be just as quick on his feet, if not quicker, and caught her from behind? Wasn't that what had likely occurred with some of his other victims who'd had the same mis-calculation?

Madison had never had any formal martial arts training. But she had learned some hand-to-hand combat and defensive tactics during basic training. Moreover, her law enforcement family members had taught her a thing or two about survival skills. If she didn't make use of them now, when would she ever?

"Since you're going to kill me anyway," Madison said to the Blue Ridge Parkway Killer as he got closer, "can you at least find a way to pass along to my family that I loved them with all my heart?"

Deschanel seemed taken aback by the odd request but replied, "Yeah, sure, I'll do that for you, Ranger Lynley."

In the split second of time she was afforded, Madison noted that he had lowered the knife just enough to give her a window of opportunity to strike him before he could cut her. Balling her fist, she drew her arm back as far as she could before thrusting it forward with all her might. The fist landed squarely in the middle of his nose. The sound of bone cracking was quickly drowned out by the howl of pain that erupted from his mouth like an injured wolf.

During this distraction from his deadly intentions, Madison tried to grab her pistol from Deschanel's waist. But he was somehow able to recover enough to slice the knife across her wrist and throw her hard to the ground in one swift motion.

"You'll pay for breaking my nose," he spat, wiping

away blood streaming down his face and neck. "You're going to die a horrific death, Ranger!"

Madison bit back the discomfort from her cut wrist and sucked in a deep breath as she wondered if his frightening forecast of her impending death was about to come true as he raised the knife threateningly with every intention of adding her to his three-decades-long list of victims.

Chapter Nineteen

When he'd spotted Madison's Tahoe in the parking lot of the Raven Rocks Overlook, alongside a Land Rover, Garrett didn't wait for the results of the run on the license plate of the Land Rover. By the time he had reached the area beneath the overlook and gathered with rangers and sheriff's deputies, Garrett had verified over his cell phone that the vehicle was registered to Ronnie Mantegna, the alias for serial killer Bryan Deschanel. It was clear to Garrett that Deschanel was intent on repeating history, dating back three decades, with Madison to be his latest victim.

I can't let that happen, Garrett had told himself with determination, as he removed the service pistol from his shoulder holster. He'd ordered everyone to spread out in search of Madison and the murder suspect in the woods. When Maintenance Ranger Ward Wilcox was found barely conscious but alive, having been shot in the chest, he fingered Ronnie Mantegna as his shooter and confirmed that he had taken Madison.

At least she was still alive, Garrett felt, as he'd zeroed in on the area he suspected Deschanel planned to make his move. It was the spot where the murderer had taken the life of Garrett's mother so many years ago. When rangers and law enforcement converged on the wooded location, Garrett gulped as he saw Deschanel holding a knife to Madison.

Just as it seemed like the perp would stab her before they could stop him, Madison delivered a head-snapping fist to Deschanel's nose. She attempted to reach for her gun that he had taken, but Deschanel appeared to slice her wrist and throw Madison down to the ground. As Garrett approached the culprit, who was holding the serrated knife in an offensive posture, he literally shot the weapon right out of Deschanel's hand, taking away a finger at the same time.

When Deschanel went for Madison's gun, Garrett tackled him, and the firearm fell harmlessly to the ground. Atop the criminal, he slugged him once in the jaw and another hard shot to his bloodied nose, causing the man to whine like a baby.

"You're under arrest, Bryan Deschanel," Garrett voiced sternly, "for the murder of Jessica Sneed, the attempted murder of Law Enforcement Ranger Madison Lynley, and a number of other crimes you'll have to answer to."

Resisting the strong urge to pummel his mother's murderer as payback, Garrett instead remembered that he was an NPS ISB special agent, bound by the law above all else, and climbed off. He turned him over to the Buncombe County Sheriff for processing, and Deschanel was promptly placed under arrest.

Garrett immediately raced to Madison, who was on her feet, her wrist bleeding. "Paramedics are on their way," he told her, having taken preemptive steps in requesting medical assistance during the drive to the parkway, in case needed.

"It's not that bad, really," she insisted.

"Bad enough to need stitches."

She grinned and glanced at Deschanel as he was being escorted away. "You should see the other guy."

"I already did." Garrett laughed. "Glad you were able to soften him up a bit for me to finish the job."

She chuckled, masking her discomfort. "Hey, that's what teamwork is all about, right?"

"Right." He hugged her, careful not to press against her wrist, while feeling grateful that she hadn't been killed. "Other than the cut, did he hurt you?"

Madison touched the side of her head. "Come to think of it, Ronnie Mantegna—er, Bryan Deschanel—did knock me unconscious when I wasn't looking to bring me to this spot."

Garrett shuddered. "All the more reason to get you to the hospital to be checked out."

"I suppose."

He was handed a piece of cloth by a park ranger to tie around her wrist to stop the bleeding. "That should do the trick," he said, knowing it couldn't take the place of stitches. Or painkillers.

"Thanks." She looked at Garrett sadly. "Deschanel confessed to killing your mother in this area."

Garrett's brow creased, feeling maudlin. "I guessed

that was why he brought you here. Some sick kind of history repeating itself."

"Speaking of which, Deschanel also confessed to killing his own mother and getting away with it," Madison told him as they headed out of the woods, "along with stabbing to death Vicki Flanagan the following year, near the Yadkin Valley Overlook. He was practically giddy at the idea that Blake O'Donnell had taken the rap for the murder."

"Not surprised by any of that," Garrett muttered, having already come to the conclusion that Deschanel had been responsible for both murders. "His depravity apparently knows no bounds."

"I agree." Madison made a face. "He also took full credit as the Blue Ridge Parkway Killer. Plus one, with the murder of Ward Wilcox." Her mouth twisted mournfully.

"We can subtract one." Garrett watched her carefully for any signs of a concussion from the blow to Madison's head. Or loss of blood. "Wilcox is still alive. He was shot in the chest but is expected to pull through."

"Thank goodness." She sighed. "Ward was an innocent pawn in Deschanel's scheming and tried to warn me, but it was too late."

"Actually, Wilcox was right on time," Garrett told her. "Before losing consciousness, he confirmed that you were still alive when he last saw you and that you were with Deschanel."

She nodded appreciatively.

They reached the Raven Rocks Overlook just as

the paramedics arrived. "You were right to believe that one unsub was responsible for serial murders over three decades," Madison pointed out.

"Yeah, bittersweet." Garrett frowned. He took no great joy in making the right call of solving a cold and current case at once. It still wouldn't bring back his mother. Or the other four women to die by Bryan Deschanel's hand, for that matter. But it would allow all the surviving family and friends of the victims some closure. Himself included.

Right now, he was just happy to know that Madison had lived to see another day. Hopefully many days. Days they could spend together. But first was for Madison to be given a clean bill of health as she got in the ambulance after her ordeal with a ruthless serial killer.

THAT EVENING, Madison was at her mountain chalet resting, her wrist sewn and wrapped, headache barely noticeable, and relieved that she was alive and the nightmare over. Once he recovered from a broken nose, jaw and one less finger, serial killer Bryan Deschanel would be headed to jail. But as much as she wanted to focus on the satisfaction of knowing that the death of Jessica Sneed had at long last been solved and her son could put this cold case to rest on a personal and professional level, Madison's current thoughts centered on what their own future held. Garrett, as attentive as he had been all day, catering to her every need to make sure she was comfortable, had been strangely silent as to where his head was. Was he deliberately trying to drive her mad? Make her question that she was reading what they had correctly? Or was he still indecisive as to what he wanted and with whom? Only to decide that it might be time to put in for another transfer, rather than deal with tender matters of the heart?

As they sat on her midcentury sofa watching television, Madison decided it was time to lay her cards— or heart—on the proverbial table. She grabbed the remote from the glass top of the coffee table, cut off the television, and turned to Garrett before asking, "So, did you mean it?"

He faced her. "Mean it?"

"That you loved me?" She held his gaze. "You said that when…"

"I know when I said it." Garrett flashed a thoughtful grin, pausing. "I meant it, every word."

Her heart fluttered. "You never followed up on those deep words of affection."

"That's because I was waiting for the right time to do so," he claimed.

She batted her lashes. "You mean when I had to pry it out of you?"

He chuckled. "Not exactly."

Madison was confused. "Care to explain?"

"Okay." Garrett turned his body to face hers. "After our last attempt at a relationship went south, I was determined to make sure that this time around we wouldn't find a way to pull away from each other. That included allowing the relationship to grow at its own pace. Without the pressures that came with premature declarations of love. The last thing I wanted was to scare you off."

"That would never have happened," she insisted.

"Never say never," he stated wisely. "Except when it comes to knowing that I don't want to spend the rest of my life with anyone but you, Madison."

Her eyes lit. "You mean that?"

"With all my heart." He took her uninjured hand, which happened to be the one with the wedding-ring finger. "The truth is it scared the hell of out me when I thought for even an instant that Bryan Deschanel might have taken you away from me. I knew then that I never wanted to let you get away again. This evening was about giving you some time to heal and reflect, without having you believe that my asking for your hand in marriage was borne out of some sense of duty because of what Deschanel nearly got away with. Or as a doing right by my mother homage of some sort as the type of woman I imagine she would have loved for me to marry and be a mother-in-law to. While that last part is true, I want you as my bride strictly because I'm madly in love with you and want us to make the most of the years ahead, as husband and wife." He sucked in a calming breath. "So, with all that being said, Madison Lynley, will you marry me and make this special agent the happiest man on this planet?"

"Hmm…" She hesitated. "And where would we live as a married couple?"

"Wherever you'd like," he answered smoothly. "The great thing about working for the National

Park Service and having the experience to back it up, with over four hundred individual national park units spread across the country and US territories, we can pretty much live anywhere we choose to."

"Good point," she had to admit.

"As for a ring, it's been on the back of my mind, but I hadn't really homed in on it," Garrett said and leaned his face to one side. "Been a bit preoccupied of late, you know?"

Madison laughed. "Excuses, excuses."

He gave her a serious look. "So, is that a yes?"

She pretended to think about it for a moment or two, then answered unequivocally, "Of course it's a yes! Yes, I'll marry you, Garrett Sneed."

He beamed. "Yeah?"

"Yes, with pleasure." She flashed her teeth. "Oh, and just for the record, I would have gladly married you wherever we lived and even without a ring, if that's what it took to get you down the aisle." Madison regarded him in earnest. "I love you, Garrett, and want to get to know more about your culture, and you can learn whatever you don't already know about my family."

"We'll have a lifetime to accomplish that and much more, Madison," he promised. "Why don't we seal the deal with a kiss?"

"Say no more," she answered him, lifting her chin up and moving toward his lips for a long, deal-sealing kiss to warm the heart and soul.

Epilogue

A week later, Garrett happily placed a three-stone 18-karat rose-gold engagement ring on Madison's finger, thrilled to see her light up with this reflection of his love and commitment to her. He looked forward to a repeat performance when it was time to place the wedding band on her finger next year.

The following spring, they went jogging on the Boone Fork Trail off the Blue Ridge Parkway on a warm day. The five-and-a-half-mile loop trek was a habit Garrett had gotten used to during their off time from their National Park Service duties, after deciding to make their home together in the Blue Ridge Mountains. They meandered their way through the woods, abundant with rhododendrons and lush meadows, and spied Carolina ducks swimming in Boone Fork Creek.

"Bryan Deschanel was transferred to Central Prison," Garrett mentioned of the close-custody male prison in Raleigh.

Madison looked at him. "Really?"

"Yeah. Guess he got into some kind of skirmish

at Piedmont Correctional Institution and was moved elsewhere from Salisbury for his own safety."

"Hmm…" She drew a breath. "As long as they keep him locked up for good."

"You can be sure of that," Garrett told her. He thought about the evidence that had helped bring Bryan Deschanel down. In retesting the survival knife that had killed Jessica Sneed, a forensic unknown DNA profile had been discovered that had proved to be a match for Bryan Deschanel's DNA. He'd been linked as well to the murders of Olivia Forlani and Nicole Wallenberg through his right-hand palm print that had matched the latent palm print from the survival knife used to stab to death the women. Lastly, DNA from murder victim Heidi Ushijima had been found on the same serrated knife that Deschanel had used to cut Madison, tying him to at least four murders and one attempted murder. He'd separately tried to kill Ward Wilcox with Madison's Sig Sauer pistol.

With the solid case against him, Deschanel had pled guilty to avoid the death penalty and had been given a life sentence without the possibility of parole. The $50,000 reward that had led to the serial killer's arrest and conviction had been awarded to Neil Novak. He and his daughter, Dominique, had been true to their word in donating the entire sum to female victims of violent crime groups.

Madison grabbed Garrett's hand and brought them to a stop. "Your mother would be proud of you."

"You're probably right." He was thoughtful, wishing she had been around to see him now. "That would have to begin with being smart enough to fall in love with the right person."

"Is that so?" She blushed, lashes fluttering wildly. "Just how smart are you?"

Garrett took her shoulders and said sweetly to Madison, "Sometimes, actions speak louder than words." With that, he gave her a searing kiss and knew their love was pure genius.

* * * * *

Don't miss the next title in R. Barri Flowers's miniseries The Lynleys of Law Enforcement when Cold Murder in Kolton Lake *goes on sale next month!*

And if you missed the previous books in the series, look for Special Agent Witness *and* Christmas Lights Killer, *available now!*

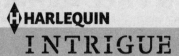
#2205 BIG SKY DECEPTION
Silver Stars of Montana • by BJ Daniels
Sheriff Brandt Parker knows that nothing short of her father's death could have lured Molly Lockhart to Montana. He's determined to protect the stubborn, independent woman but keeping his own feelings under control is an additional challenge as his investigation unfolds.

#2206 WHISPERING WINDS WIDOWS
Lookout Mountain Mysteries • by Debra Webb
Lucinda was angry when her husband left his job in the city to work with his father. Deidre never shared her husband's dream of moving to Nashville. And Harlowe wanted a baby that her husband couldn't give her. When their men vanished, the Whispering Winds Widows told the same story. Will the son of one of the disappeared and a writer from Chattanooga finally uncover the truth?

#2207 K-9 SHIELD
New Mexico Guard Dogs • by Nichole Severn
Jones Driscoll has spent half his life in war zones. This rescue mission feels different. Undercover journalist Maggie Caddel is tough—and yet she still rouses his instinct to protect. She might trust him to help her bring down the cartel that held her captive, but neither of them has any reason to let down their guards and trust the connection they share.

#2208 COLD MURDER IN KOLTON LAKE
The Lynleys of Law Enforcement • by R. Barri Flowers
Reviewing a cold case, FBI special agent Scott Lynley needs the last person to see the victim alive. Still haunted by his aunt's death, FBI victim specialist Abby Zhang is eager to help. Yet even two decades later, someone is putting Abby in the cross fire of the Kolton Lake killer. Scott's mission is to solve the case but Abby's quickly becoming his first—and only—priority.

#2209 THE RED RIVER SLAYER
Secure One • by Katie Mettner
When a fourth woman is found dead in a river, security expert Mack Holbock takes on the search for a cunning serial killer. A disabled vet, Mack is consumed by guilt that's left him with no room or desire for love. But while investigating and facing danger with Charlotte—a traumatized victim of sex trafficking—he must protect her and win her trust...without falling for her.

#2210 CRASH LANDING
by Janice Kay Johnson
After surviving a crash landing and the killers gunning for them, Rafe Salazar and EMS paramedic Gwen Allen are on the run together. Hunted across treacherous mountain wilderness, Gwen has no choice but to trust her wounded patient—a DEA agent on a dangerous undercover mission. Vowing to keep each other safe even as desire draws them closer, will they live to fight another day?